The Beauty and the Hell of It

& Other Stories

Lynda Williams

GUERNICA
EDITIONS
TORONTO • CHICAGO • BUFFALO • LANCASTER (U.K.)
2025

Guernica Founder: Antonio D'Alfonso

Michael Mirolla, general editor
Julie Roorda, editor
David Moratto, interior and cover design

Guernica Editions Inc.
1241 Marble Rock Rd., Gananoque, ON K7G 2V4
2250 Military Road, Tonawanda, N.Y. 14150-6000 U.S.A.
www.guernicaeditions.com

Distributors:
Independent Publishers Group (IPG)
600 North Pulaski Road, Chicago IL 60624
University of Toronto Press Distribution (UTP)
5201 Dufferin Street, Toronto (ON), Canada M3H 5T8

First edition.
Printed in Canada.

Legal Deposit—Third Quarter
Library of Congress Catalog Card Number: 2024945668
Library and Archives Canada Cataloguing in Publication
Title: The beauty and the hell of it : & other stories / Lynda Williams.
Other titles: Beauty and the hell of it (Compilation)
Names: Williams, Lynda (Author of The beauty and the hell of it), author.
Series: Essential prose series ; 230.
Description: Series statement: Essential prose series ; 230
Identifiers: Canadiana (print) 20240452755 | Canadiana (ebook)
20240454820 | ISBN 9781771839686 (softcover) |
ISBN 9781771839693 (EPUB)
Subjects: LCGFT: Short stories.
Classification: LCC PS8645.I4528 B43 2025 | DDC C813/.6—dc23

Essential Prose Series 230

Canada Council for the Arts
Conseil des arts du Canada

ONTARIO ARTS COUNCIL
CONSEIL DES ARTS DE L'ONTARIO

an Ontario government agency
un organisme du gouvernement de l'Ontario

Canada

Guernica Editions Inc. acknowledges the support of the Canada Council for the Arts and the Ontario Arts Council. The Ontario Arts Council is an agency of the Government of Ontario.

We acknowledge the financial support of the Government of Canada.

In Praise of *The Beauty and the Hell of It*

Prepare to fall in love with this cast of messy, irreverent women, stumbling on the sidelines of their loved ones' rites of adulthood. There may be three weddings and a funeral here (and one christening, one child's birthday party, countless deaths and a broken engagement), but you will not find romance. With wry humour, sparse prose, and heart-stopping bluntness, Lynda Williams allows us into the damaged, tender hearts of women who colour outside the lines.
—Susan Sanford Blades, author of *Fake It So Real*

Lynda Williams is one of the most brilliant and incisive authors I've read, and *The Beauty and the Hell of It* is one hell of a collection. Like the love child of Mary Gaitskill and Lorrie Moore, Williams' stories are full of sharp observations, complex emotions and sly humour. From the opening story, "Matches," to the final, title story, each one is deeply felt, and full of innovation and subversion. Savour each beautifully-crafted sentence and paragraph; these stories will stay with you for a long time.
—Danila Botha, author of *Things that Cause Inappropriate Happiness* and *A Place for People Like Us*

Lynda Williams is possessed of that rarest and most important of gifts, an original voice. What's more, she has guts. Throughout her growing body of work, she refuses to shy away from tough topics. That said, the energy and wit of her writing allow her to delve into the dark side of human experience without losing the reader to despair. Her characters are complex human beings driven by compelling needs and desires.
—Alissa York, author of *Far Cry*

There are some stories in here that, after I read them, I have to sit quietly for a while, maybe a day or two, maybe much longer, and think about what I've experienced in the reading. These are the stories of women who dissect their sorrows with an intellect like scissors, and survive their struggles like soldiers making light of war. And despite the pain I feel in the telling, I still find myself laughing alongside; it's how they brought me in to share their lives.
—Richard Harrison, author of *On Not Losing My Father's Ashes in the Flood*, Winner of the Governor General's Literary Award

For Heather,
and in loving memory of Sean Murray Connell
(July 10, 1983–July 4, 2010)

Contents

Matches

Ten hours before my sister's wedding, I decide to paint the bedroom green. Of all the decisions I have made in the past six months, this one is most sound.

I live in a double-wide trailer, hidden in the middle of an uncultivated sugar bush in the Eastern Townships. My bedroom has a single north-facing window. The room is cold and dark and great for sleeping. Mediocre for making love. The mattress is iffy and the only electrical outlet needs repair, so no mood lighting. You can fumble in the dark or cringe under the fluorescents.

I prefer the kitchen table.

The closet has no doors. It did at one point, but they were sliding and stupid, so I took them off after my husband's funeral. Matt did the same thing for me with the cupboards in the kitchen. I like the labels peeking out at me while I scramble eggs in the morning. So far, everything I've done with the house is poor and white and trashy. I'm in a hurry for the porch to rot. I want the UPS guy—who barks back at my Rottweiler when he thinks I'm not there—to slip and fall. Then I'll let Lucy off her chain.

"I was thinking something *sage-ish*, you know? Sort of neutral. Nothing minty that would remind you of a nursery or toothpaste."

The orange-apron clad sales clerk reaches for her samples. Her furrowed unibrow lets me know my need for assistance has ruined her day. Surely this is why we all go to Home Depot. You can do it. We *could* help.

Matt motions to me that he will be in the tool department. I place my foot over his undone shoelace. He folds his arms across his chest. I do the same.

I read the headline to the news story that recounted Scott's death—*Fatal Crash Kills Two*—standing ankle-deep in mud beside the mailbox at the end of the drive. Then I walked back to the house and tore apart the closet searching for his Louisville slugger. Now my paper gets delivered to a knothole in an elm beside the road.

Both drivers died on impact. The car wasn't his. He was supposed to be in New York, on business. The passenger was his secretary.

I haven't thought about moving all the furniture. I'm trying to decide if I should wear heels to the wedding, and I realize I will be expected to say something. Something nice. And then, next week, I'll have to listen to twelve different accounts of exactly how nice it was from all the ladies at the bank. I can hear them. And the organ. This has my full attention. Matt, who is trying to maneuver the queen-sized mattress out the door, does not.

"You sure you wanna do this today?"

"Of course!" It comes out with a hint of desperation. I have done more crying than sleeping in this room over the last six months.

Someone—probably one of those kind women who sent the casseroles, the same ones who dropped their eyes each time I said *hello* when we crossed paths in town before he died—once told me that death eclipses infidelity. My mother was more upfront about it. She took me aside before the service and said, "People expect you to be sad dear, not angry."

My husband's funeral was every bit as elaborate as our wedding. His family took care of everything, and they all sat on the same side of the church. She had enough sense not to show up at the service, but I picked her out at the burial, hiding behind a pair of oversized Dolce and Gabbana sunglasses. Pointless really, when you have your arm done up in a sling.

I caught up with her under a willow near the cemetery gates. I needed a closer look at what Scott had traded me in for.

"How did you know my husband?"

She stiffened. Silence yawned between us until she finally said, "From work," with that velvety 1-900 voice I was acquainted with from the phone. She took a step to move away and I seized her in a vice-like embrace. Who knew a hug could be so vindicating? I wanted to snap off her limbs like drumsticks, to make a feast out of my husband's leftovers. I'd spit out those tiny diamond studs like watermelon seeds. Were they a gift from Scott? For all I knew, she had a husband waiting at home with all the same questions I had.

"Thank you for coming," I whispered. "It means so much." I gave her one last squeeze and walked away wondering what man could resist her giant nostrils and Chiclet teeth.

Matt made it home for the last of the Wild Turkey. He put the handbrake on the truck, hugged me, and held my hair back while I threw up. Lucy sniffed my puke on his boots, I put clean sheets on the bed, and Matt poured the entire contents of my liquor cabinet down the sink. We've been limping along like a family ever since.

Once the room is empty and our voices echo in its hollowness, we start masking. Matt runs tape along the ceiling and door-frame. I do the baseboards and window. I like hearing the steady rip and stick of the tape. I could do this all day. I could tape an entire wall. Make designs. Splash paint over little rips in the tape. And when I wake up from a horrible dream, I could scratch at the walls until all the tape is in a ball that I could step on and kick, or just throw away. I could roll over and go to sleep afterward. Paint my room again the next day.

I pry the lid off the can with a screwdriver. Matt removes the switch plate.

He says, "You're going to be sorry you didn't use primer. Or a drop cloth."

I say, "I've made worse mistakes."

I dip the virgin wood of the paint stick into the bucket of Sico, painfully aware that it will be permanently changed, the coating it acquires impossible to remove. I should be doing this with my sister.

I reach for the tray and pour.

"Shit."

Three drops of sage spill onto the linoleum.

Screw it. They can stay. This room needs latex teardrops.

I dip the lemon yellow roller into the paint, saturate it with my beautiful sage green, then I roll it back and forth across the top of the tray to remove the excess. I like the sound of the roller even better than the tape.

I make two boring streaks across the wall. Take a step back. Go over the streaks again. This won't work without primer. I drop the roller and reach for the can, splash the remainder of its contents against the wall. It sounds like vomit hitting the pavement at the bottom of the rollercoaster. It looks smoother. I watch it pool on the floor. It is the best forty dollars I have ever spent.

Matt cracks his neck. Probably to remind me he's there.

We stare at each other for a minute, then I wipe my hands on the front of my shirt.

"I call the shower."

* * *

Tugging my hair into a French knot, I contemplate the toast. I feel like following Thumper's advice that saying nothing at all would be the safest option. Could I get away with a succinct *To the bride and groom*? Or do I give in to the temptation to share some of the hard-earned wisdom from my two plus years of marriage? Why didn't anyone stand up at my wedding to say, "Don't let the sun go down on your anger," or "Don't let leaving his dirty socks on the coffee table be the hill you choose to die on." Did all the practical advice dissolve with the open bar? Did they forsake us because we held the reception at a golf course, or because we served chicken instead of roast beef?

Here's what I know: you don't get married because it's time, because that's what your friends are doing, because you've been dating an accountant with chiseled features and a devastating mouth, like Gavin Rossdale's. You don't have to say yes because someone offers you a ring.

I've heard it said that the only people who really know what goes on in a marriage are the two parties involved. This assumes that you're seated at a table for two. I thought I belonged to a partnership. Turns out it was more like Mr. and Mrs. Enright Incorporated. I thought I had a husband who was committed to his job. I thought he commuted to Montreal everyday because I didn't want to move to the city. There are people who believe that I had to know, that it was impossible not to, but people who are married aren't necessarily known to each other any more than we know ourselves.

I need more bobby pins. I can't expect my Big and Sexy hairspray to do all the work.

* * *

Behind the church, I chain-smoke Export A green label. I am not a smoker. Not since college. I don't even have a lighter. Matt strikes a match to light each one, watching the flame burn down to his fingertips.

"You look good with your hair up."

I blow a wreath of smoke. "You look good when you shave."

The corner of his mouth lifts into a smile. "Are you trying to tell me something?"

The smoke catches in my throat. I cough. "I just did."

I tap the ash off the end of my cigarette. Watch the breeze carry it away. October is a lousy month for a wedding. Wet and grey and cold. Today isn't any of those things. I swear the wedding planner tore this day out of a mail-order catalogue.

Matt leans his head toward the door. "Ready?"

I shake my head. "One more." I can see his frown without even looking.

"Why don't you save it for after the ceremony?"

"I'll buy another pack."

He pulls a face. "You'll be sick. I'm not sitting beside you. You're not throwing up in my lap during a toast."

"I don't need your lap." It's all I can do to keep my hand from shaking as I bring the cigarette to my mouth. "I have a purse."

This town has enough to say about me without seeing the contents of my stomach emptied expertly into a velvet clutch, but I need to stay behind the church. I need an excuse not to smile and greet all the hen-pecking gossips who want to say how *are* you dear. At least they can't say I've gone downhill. I'm tall and slim and my legs are more than long enough to wrap securely around a man's thirty-two-inch waist. I haven't gained or lost a pound in the last year. The only thing that's changed is my hair. I grew it out. And damned if it doesn't look better, too.

Most people can't figure why he'd cheat on a fox like me. I have an idea though, but only because he accused me of screwing every bartender, mechanic, and salesman I met.

"Did I ever tell you about our honeymoon?"

"No, you never—"

"That's right. You were in Fort Mac." I offer him the cigarette, and after a pause he takes it.

"So we got a deal on tickets to Puerto Vallarta. We settled for a cheap motel. Figured we'd spend all our time on the beach. *Right.* I got food poisoning from the chicken salad sandwich I ate on the plane. I spent half our time there hugging the toilet while roaches crawled over my feet."

"And he?"

"Drank tequila on the beach."

Matt takes a drag on the cigarette and passes it back to me. He waves to the O'Ridans as they hobble toward the church. I paste on my smile. It's thin and short-lived and lets you know that I own a Rottweiler.

"They're probably talking about us."

"Yeah? What do you think they're saying?"

"That I'm a wid-*hoe* and you're more than a handyman and you shouldn't be living with me. What with my poor husband barely cold in the grave."

For a minute, everything is quiet. Even the wind takes a pause from rustling in the leaves. Matt fiddles with the matchbook, opening and closing the cover and opening it again until it's ready to fall apart.

"He'll cheat you forever if you let him."

"What?"

He taps my nose with the tip of his index finger. "You've still got paint on your face."

I rub my nose and replace the green with angry red. "Better?"

He nods and leaves me to find my own way inside the church.

I can feel the grease of the tar and nicotine coating my tongue. My throat is raw from the smoke. In just a few hours, I'll have to stand up and make that toast. I don't have words. My eyes drop and blur. I notice something pink on the ground.

The matchbook. It looks familiar. Like I should find one inside my own wallet. The silver script on the cover reads, "AGHS Grads of 1996."

High school prom. We must have collected a dozen of those matchbooks that night.

Because we were bored.

Because we could.

Because we were losers.

Twelve years later, I have the same date and he's wearing the same suit.

Down the cobblestone walk, I see my sister and father making their way to the church. As they approach, I notice that her hair is down and she's not wearing makeup. Her dress is off-white. Strapless. Cut just below the knee. Free of embroidery and lace. Probably bamboo.

She looks stunning.

I meet them halfway. We hug and I want to be at home hugging Lucy. Lucy wags her tail, or hides it, to let me know what she means.

"Nervous?"

She nods yes, but I can tell she's lying. She holds the yellow roses steady, without trembling. She won't drop the ring or draw a blank mid-sentence as she says her vows. She'll wait for the minister's permission to kiss. She won't trip.

"What's that?" She eyes the slip of pink twitching in my hands involuntarily.

“This?” I consider the matchbook for a second before tucking it inside my purse. “Just something I found.” I touch my nose where the spot of paint had been. “Something worth keeping.”

Then I climb the steps and hold open the door to the church.

Jesus and Jockeys

I had to decide what to do with Jesus. Take him home in the backseat of my Versa, or carry him outside and place him beside the triple duty Glad bags at the end of the drive.

I knew I was in trouble when I discovered the drawer with all the Jockey underwear. There must have been at least a dozen unopened packages. Three to a pack. All white and French cut. I could hear her extolling the virtues of cotton from the grave. Say what you will about my mother, she understood the value of fabric that breathes.

As it turned out, the entire dresser was filled with unopened packages of socks and underwear, with the exception of one small drawer devoted to greeting cards that dated back to the eighties. As someone who does not send greeting cards lest I burden someone I care about with the task of throwing them out, I believe it would be more efficient if we all just agreed to place five dollars in the garbage can and think good thoughts. And then there are people like my mother, who hold on to the gesture by warehousing it in a drawer they never open until it's time for someone else to swallow it with a trash bag.

Death changes the way you think about stuff. Everything you keep is a decision someone else is going to have to make. All those photographs that never made it into an album, the snapshots of birthdays capturing celebrations composed of cone hats, party streamers, and the Jos Louis with the single candle in the centre my mother called birthday cake. The music albums, records of Roy Orbison and mixed cassette tapes of Charley Pride and Keith Whitley, all rendered obsolete in a world that's gone digital. All the shit that haunts me more than my memories.

People shouldn't be allowed to grow old in the house they grew up in. If we all just kept moving every three to five years, like my sister and I did, no one would get caught in the layers of dead people's unmade decisions. My father's coveralls and pearl snap shirts were still hanging in the hall closet, and my grandmother's embroidery patterns and cigar boxes stuffed with thread were collecting dust on the bookcase. Those stupid hobbies meant to keep you young will put grey hairs on someone else's head.

I had inherited the job of cleaning out this place in preparation for the sale of the house mostly because I was the sister not on bed rest for the final trimester of her pregnancy. Sherri was going to have her first kid in a couple of months, and she was racing to finish the second draft of her latest novel before her due date. She wrote romances, you know, the ones with the red spines and covers featuring the long-haired Zeus-type guy with the unbuttoned shirt, and the oddly hairless chest. Of course, Sherri wasn't responsible for the ridiculous covers. She just wrote the stories, and she was working furiously to get this one done. I wanted to tell her to rest while she could, but I don't think she would have listened.

Harlequin romances were one of my mother's pleasures. The attic was filled with apple crates of them, mostly sourced for fifty cents from garage sales. At that price, I don't understand why she didn't just read them and throw them out. I asked Sherri if she wanted me to set them aside for her, but she assured me she'd probably read most of them as a teenager, so all I had to do was dispose of them. It sounds easy, but I had to haul sixteen apple crates down the narrow attic stairs in the sweltering August heat with the sound of dead mouse bones randomly crunching under the cheap foam soles of my flip-flops. By the time I had finished, I vowed to buy a Kindle so my daughter would never have to do this for me. I spent the entire first afternoon in the attic, strangled by the smell of mothballs and decomposing rodents. I retreated after using my inhaler for the third time.

My mother died of heart attack, sixty-four years young, and unlike my grandmother who had spent the final years of her life applying masking tape with our names on it to every object in her house, she didn't have anything sorted. She was still sorting through the things left behind by my father and their parents. Jesus, for instance, stood facing the corner in the spare bedroom with one raised hand missing and exposed wire in its place, giving him a Captain Hook vibe. My father, who did not so much as attend mass at Christmas, insisted it was necessary to keep him; he bent the wire on the missing hand so it would hold his pipe. It was my mother who turned him to face the corner after he passed away.

I had told Sherri from the outset that I could whip the house into shape in a week. She laughed and said, "Bring a shovel." And there I was, twenty-four hours in and beginning to see her point. I didn't visit my mother as frequently as she had, twenty minutes on the phone once a week seemed to be the limit of our tolerance for each other, and when I did come around, I rarely went past the kitchen. I couldn't remember the last time I'd been upstairs, and I was certain I hadn't been to the attic since I'd played hide-and-seek as a child. A week was a conservative estimate, but it was all the time I had. I needed to be back in the city to pick up Crystal from her dad's by six on Sunday night.

I started the new day with the spare bedroom because it would be easy—a couple of chests with empty drawers and a few good dresses in the closet. Instead I faced an obscene quantity of Jockey underwear. I took a closer look at one of the packages. The price tag was from Zellers. As I stood there judging my mother, I realized that I was wearing a bra I bought before I got married eight years ago. The elastic was shot, the straps kept slipping down, and the exposed underwire poked into my chest. It wasn't that I didn't have enough money to afford a new bra, it was just that I knew I'd need that money for something more important. I had a kid. So birthdays and Christmas and shit. Was this how my mother spent her pension? Did she walk into the store one day and decide to fill her shopping cart, or did she just pick up a pair every time she went in for a bag of Whiskas?

I had a system: garbage, donate, keep. Can you donate underthings? Who goes into the Sally Ann hoping to find a polka dot thong? How can you throw away so much perfectly good cotton?

I made another category called Ask Sherri.

I moved to the bathroom, opening the medicine cabinet to find a single pair of nail clippers and multiple jars of Pond's cold cream. I screwed the cap off each one because I recalled my mother hid cash in these when we were growing up. Sure enough, I was rewarded with three wadded up twenties. Most of the jars were just washed-out empties, with the exception of one that actually contained product. Washed out empties was a theme I would encounter again in the kitchen. Yogurt containers, pasta jars, hell, there were even baby food jars she used to sort her sewing notions. It all went out to the rented dumpster, and I began to worry there wouldn't be enough room for the important stuff, like the three-legged chesterfield and the random sheets of plywood propped up against the wall in the hallway.

By two p.m. I was ravenous, and I scoured the kitchen cupboards for something to eat. I settled for saltines and peanut butter, washed down with a cup of tea. Tetley tea and No Name peanut butter. That was the difference between my mother and me. Nothing but Kraft for my toast (it's not peanut butter without bears on the jar) and only the cheapest, largest bulk carton available for my orange pekoe, and of course, I used every bag twice.

I stayed to work in the kitchen after I ate because I knew what to expect. An obscene collection of margarine containers she called Tupperware and a "never-let-you-down" drawer filled with plastic cutlery, twist ties, and random bits of string. I found aspirin in three different cupboards and one drawer was devoted entirely to bread bags. I made short work of her excess, pulling out the drawers and dumping them into the trash. I was on a roll until I came to the china cabinet.

We ate our hot dogs and our bologna and our tuna casserole off Corelle, like every other working-class family from my generation, but my mother also had twelve place settings of Royal Albert American Beauty that she had received as a wedding gift from her grandparents. It was reserved for Christmas and Thanksgiving. Over the years she expanded her collection to include other patterns that she scavenged from yard sales. Lavender Rose was her favourite.

At that point I'd been listening to Conway Twitty spin on the Victrola for hours, and I caved and phoned Sherri just to hear a different voice.

"Do you want the dishes?"

"The Corelle?" She asked as if I'd offered her a dead skunk I found on the road.

"No, the fancy ones."

"In the hutch?"

"In it. On it. Around it."

"Just the ones you don't want."

"So all of it?"

"Isn't there a pattern you like?"

I would have liked to hear the sound of all that bone china hitting the bottom of the dumpster. "Nope."

"You do know it's worth money?"

So was my time. "I don't care if it's worth five hundred a setting. I've got nowhere to put it and no interest in selling it."

"Just wrap it all up and think on it. I'll take whatever you don't want."

"One more thing. Do you want your old report cards?"

"No, why? Are you keeping yours?"

"She didn't save mine."

"You just haven't found them yet."

And that was Sherri for you, believing in my mother as much as Mom believed in her.

I spent the next few hours wrapping dishes in newspapers from the stacks that could be found in every room in the house. I waited until a quarter past eight to bust into the dusty, half-empty bottle of Gibson's Finest. It was the best surprise so far, but curious. My mother didn't drink whiskey, and my father was all about the Canadian Club and Beefeater Gin. I had done two shots before a thought occurred to me about who the Gibson's was really for.

I'd grown up in the long shadow of my mother's short-lived affairs. I couldn't say how many she'd had over the years, and I'm not sure exactly when I clued in, but I knew the pattern. She'd fight with my father, storm out the house, and be gone for days at a time. It started when I was so young it didn't even occur to me to wonder where she was going. By the time I'd reached sixth grade, my classmates were calling Mr. Gauthier, our French teacher, my step-daddy or worse, Papa Gauthier. Mercifully, the school year outlasted their relations.

My father's health was in rapid decline—he died of lung cancer after a lifetime of working in an asbestos mine—which made him exponentially more miserable and increasingly cruel with his words. My mother was far from a slave to his needs, and Sherri was still too young to understand what was happening. I was his nurse that year, and I missed so much school that the question was raised whether I should repeat the seventh grade. Ultimately, math was the only subject I had to re-take, but my resentment took on unwieldy proportions, and until her death, I didn't miss a single opportunity to remind her. *It was around the time your father died. I wouldn't know. I was busy repeating math that year. Oh, I'm supposed to add up these numbers? I don't think I learned that. I must have been absent when they taught us. You need the percentage? Ask Mom. I traded my pencils for a mucous cup, remember?*

And then my father died and my mother reformed. She didn't re-marry. She didn't have boyfriends. She didn't go out. I found her sudden good behaviour tremendously annoying. Our house shrank with her in it, and I moved in with my first boyfriend when I was sixteen. He was twenty-four. Three months later I had my first abortion. I wasn't ready to ruin someone else's life. Yet. My mother never forgave me for bolting and setting a bad example for Sherri, but Sherri always did her own thing anyway, and she said herself the house was a happier place without the two of us arguing.

I took the stairs to her room two at a time. I'd been avoiding it up to then, but now I was suddenly interested in finding evidence. What tokens from lovers past had she kept? A letter, a bracelet, a half-used bottle of cologne? Maybe she had a separate cigar box devoted to each one. Inventory collected from each notch on the bed post. There had to be stuff.

Her room was a museum: an entire wall of cardboard boxes labelled Dad, the sewing machine buried under a pile of fabric (all floral and mostly cotton), and a tower of quilts as high as the mirror on her dresser. It was better that way. I didn't need to see my own reflection.

I opened the first drawer. It was filled with income tax returns from the nineties. The next one was a mix of argyle dress socks and sheer pantyhose. The third and fourth were shrines dedicated to my sister, bursting with mediocre artwork and well-written poems and stories. One random finger-painting with my name on it festered at the back, jammed behind Sherri's spiral-bound notebooks.

It was a disappointment to find so much stuff with so little meaning. I turned to the boxes that said Dad. I took one off the top and pulled back the flap. Inside, I discovered a collection of 45s: David Allan Coe, George Jones, Hank Snow. I picked up an album, drew the record from its sleeve and snapped it in two. I paused, half expecting to hear my father's roar. I tossed the pieces of broken record on the bed and directed my attention to the album cover. I had just committed a sin against the late, great George Jones. Yes indeed, he stopped loving her today. Finally. It was hard to believe my father had the capacity to appreciate such music.

My phone vibrated. Why was Sherri calling so late? Had she finally come to her senses about the dishes? Would I get to break them, too?

My brother-in-law Nate's voice cracked. "I'm with Sherri at the hospital."

"God, is she alright?"

"She's going to be."

"And the baby?"

"She had it." *It* did not bode well. People talked about newborns in terms of boys and girls, pounds and ounces. He whispered the next part just loud enough for me to hear. My niece, he told me, was stillborn.

I asked him to give Sherri a hug from me and to let her know I would come as soon as she was up for it.

I sat at the end of the bed and snapped my record halves in half again and again until I couldn't make them any smaller. I thought about how this baby already had a room filled with stuff in anticipation of its arrival. I thought about my sister coming home to the taunt of that nursery with all its receiving blankets and plush zoo animals that were meant to belong to a new little person, and how I would have to tell Crystal she wouldn't have a cousin.

Wandering back to the spare room, I longed to go back to the time when disposing of a chest full of new underwear was my biggest problem. I drove my foot into the backside of Jesus, expecting him to break apart like a hollow chocolate Easter bunny. He did not. I supposed I wasn't the first person to underestimate him. His face pierced a hole in the plaster behind the white and yellow daisy wallpaper and a crack ran down his blue and white robes. I recalled my father throwing me against that same wall while my mother was out doing God knows what, or whom. Did Jesus remember that after he forgave them?

My phone vibrated again. Sherri was asking for me. Would I come?

I imagined that the house was on fire and I had to decide what to save.

I left without locking the door and threw Jesus in the back seat of the car with my purse. I hopped into the driver's seat and took one final look in the rearview mirror. It was dark, so there wasn't much to see, which seemed fitting. I started to turn the key, but I stopped before the engine could turn over. I got out and went around back to the passenger's side to fasten the Saviour's seatbelt. I didn't want there to be any confusion about who was saving whom.

Tradition

It's December, snowy, two days before Christmas, and the first holiday since my mother died. I want to stay in bed with the covers pulled over my head until January. It seems to be working really well for our father.

"Hurry up, David! I need the shower!"

I'm pounding on the door and my brother is ignoring me. Our home, like most trailers, only has one bathroom, which means around here, yelling and grooming go together like pie and ice cream.

"I'll shit on your bed if you don't open that door in the next thirty seconds!"

The door swings open and my dumb handsome brother saunters into the hall. A wave of Axe body spray rushes out with him, threatening to choke me.

While I take a two-minute shower under all the cold water he left me, David goes outside and starts the truck. I wonder if he'll actually move the tools out of the back or just pretend to forget and let me do it in the parking lot at Superstore. Few things are less practical than bringing home two weeks' worth of groceries in the open bed of a truck, but since Dad's Buick died, that's exactly what we've been doing. It means I get to ride for twenty-five minutes with three cartons of eggs stacked on my knees. David likes to take the corners fast just to hear me scream.

"Did you bring the list?" he asks as I climb into the cab.

"Yeah, it's in my pocket."

"Good. Have you figured out what we're gonna get Dad for Christmas?"

"No idea. I thought that was your department."

He pauses to light a cigarette. "You're joking, right?"

I shrug. "You're a guy. I thought you'd know what to get."

"Fine. We'll pick up a case of beer."

"We can't give him beer for Christmas."

"Bottles, not cans. Imported. He'll drink it."

"Whatever. I'm not wrapping it."

We drive in silence for a while and I fiddle with the radio, searching for a station that isn't playing Christmas music. I settle for Merle Haggard's "If We Make It Through December."

"Why do we even need to have Christmas dinner? We could just pick up Chinese and have leftovers."

"Come on. It's not Christmas without a turkey."

"It's not Christmas without Mom."

David takes a final drag off his cigarette and tosses the butt out the window. "They're forecasting twenty-five centimetres of snow. Dad's gonna be working. He should at least come home to a decent meal."

When he's not locked in his room, my father drives a snowplow.

"And you think we're capable of providing this decent meal?"

"How hard can it be? Besides, Jessie's coming."

And suddenly my brother's enthusiasm for the season makes sense. Jessie is the older girlfriend that he tries so hard to impress. At twenty-four to his twenty-two, she's hardly a cougar, but I've never thought of David as mature, so I don't understand what she sees in him beyond a faint resemblance to Paul Walker.

Our trip into Spruce Grove is productive and uneventful, and since David and I are still on speaking terms as we unload the truck, life is good. For the moment. I'm not really excited to meet his girlfriend. My brother has been a player for as long as I can remember. I mean, I didn't even know he was capable of dating one person at a time, and then Mom dies and suddenly he's in a committed relationship? Forgive me if I don't want to meet the witch who cast that spell.

And now, because of that sorceress, I am going to spend Christmas Eve and Christmas Day entertaining. Like I even know what that means. Do I open a bag of chips? Throw coats on my bed? Or just apologize because we don't have any stemware?

I really wish David wasn't dragging me into this. Part of me thinks he's just doing it so he doesn't have to think about Mom. I'm sure he has no idea what he's getting us into.

So instead of a present, because let's face it, the gas station doesn't pay that much, I'm cooking David's favourite for supper on Christmas Eve: Mom's lasagna. If I can pull it off, it'll be a nice change from beans on toast.

* * *

"We need a tree."

I've been waiting for someone to say this. Mid-afternoon on the twenty-fourth seems about right.

"There's a Pine Fresh hanging off the rearview in the truck."

"A real one."

"Put tinsel on the aloe plant. It's real enough."

David looks at the withered plant perched on the entertainment unit.

"It's dead. Shouldn't we throw it out?"

"It was Mom's."

He gives no sign of hearing me, just absently pats his shirt pocket to make sure his cigarettes are still there.

"Where's Dad?"

"He left for work an hour ago."

"Right." He grabs his coat off the back of a chair.

"I'm going to pick up Jessie and find a tree," he frowns, "or something we can put a star on. Her brother's driving in from Edmonton. If he shows up before we're back, just make him feel at home, okay?"

"Sure. What's his name?"

"Andrew. Drew, not Andy."

"What happens if I call him Andy?"

"Just try to behave. Don't swear too much." With that he strides to the door.

"You left your keys on the table."

"Shit. Thanks." He pauses at the door and turns back toward the kitchen. "Don't let him distract you. If you burn my lasagna, I'll eat the fucker for dessert."

I give him the finger. I want to tell him to drive carefully because it's almost dark, and I need him not to hit a moose like Mom did, but that's not how we operate.

Instead, all the affection I have for my brother is concentrated in my middle finger.

It starts to snow shortly after he leaves and I wonder if anyone will be back in time for supper, or if it will just be me and a ridiculous amount of food. I've barely started on the Bolognese when I notice a stranger dragging a blue spruce up the back steps. I hear three short raps at the door. I open it for a man who is actually taller than the tree. I'm not sure which is more impressive, the man or the evergreen, and I can feel the words *Holy Fuck* tingling on my lips.

"You must be David's sister. I'm Drew, Jessie's brother." And because I'm staring blankly he adds, "Were you expecting me?"

No, I was not expecting a lumberjack. "Come in. David mentioned that you were on your way. I just wasn't expecting you so soon, or um, that."

He ducks his head to clear the door. "I would have been here sooner if it wasn't for the tree. I was five clicks out when Jessie texted me to find one, and not to show up at all if I didn't."

My eyes wander over the spruce, snow dripping off its branches and a bird's nest still stuck inside. I try to hide my smile. "I think I'm going to like your sister."

"Hard not to, I promise. Where should I put this?"

"Why don't you just lean it against the wall here while I move the couch?"

By the time I've pulled out all the decorations and Drew and I have exchanged awkward pleasantries that dwindle into awkward silence, David and Jessie finally show up. I've never been so relieved to see him.

I have to say, she's not what I expected. She's a short brunette with a pointy chin and thick eyebrows. She's delicate and petite, but her voice is deep and husky, like Captain Hook trapped inside Tinkerbell's body. She gives her brother a thumbs-up when she notices the tree.

I head back to the kitchen, but not before noticing Jessie give Drew a hug. I try to picture myself hugging David, but I can't. We're not that kind of family.

I overhear him talking to Jessie in the living room. "Do you know anything about cooking turkey?"

She assures him she has never cooked anything that didn't involve a microwave and a can opener.

"Is it thawed?" This from Drew. He wins the turkey preparation lottery through experience.

I leave the lasagna under the broiler too long, and the cheese comes out overdone. No one complains. Normally when I cook food that doesn't turn out, David chastises me by saying, "You forgot to put the love in it," but I guess he's behaving for his girlfriend. We all clean up the kitchen together, which seems strange. I don't think I've ever seen my brother pick up a dish towel. To snap it at the back of my legs, sure, all the time, but never for its intended purpose. Also, Jessie is being super nice, asking questions to get to know me, and this feels weird, too. Usually the women in David's life can't be bothered. I'm just the chubby younger sister they get to wrinkle their noses at. Best case scenario I get ignored, and that's how I prefer it. I don't know what to do with this attention. I actually have to follow the conversation because someone might ask me what I think.

Once the kitchen is tidy, we decorate the tree. Since when has my brother ever cared about hanging ornaments?

He's not the one with all the memories of doing this with Mom. He probably doesn't even realize it has to be taken down. It's one more thing I'll be stuck doing alone.

Finally, we all gather in front of the television to watch *It's a Wonderful Life*. I can't help but think this would be a different movie if that Mary woman didn't smile so damn much. I can't believe David is pretending to be into this crap. Normally on Christmas Eve, we watch a marathon of *The Fast and the Furious*. We know all the lines. I could cut my eyes at David at any moment and he'd give me his best Dom Toretto. None this "an angel gets its wings" garbage.

After the movie, while we're all yawning and stretching, David pulls a velvet box from his shirt pocket and hands it to Jessie. She flips the top to find the tiniest diamond winking back at her. He takes the ring and says, "Will you marry me?"

The look on her face is like watching a storm in a snow globe, every emotion all at once, and finally all of them eclipsed by surprise. I cast a look toward Drew to see if he's as shocked as his sister, only to discover that he is watching me, gauging my reaction.

I want to flip him off because I hate him for not being caught off guard, but I bite my thumbnail. If Jessie has given David an answer, I haven't heard, so I just stand up and say, "Congratulations you two. I'm going to bed."

Most things I can handle: my father's drinking binges and his inability to parent, my brother's promiscuous habits, not having a mother anymore, but this is fucked up. It's my job to be happy for David, and maybe this is good, but all I can think is he's leaving me. Alone with my Dad and Jack Daniels. So once the house is quiet and everyone is tucked into bed, I sit up on the counter in the bathroom and cut my wrist open over the sink. Just enough blood to make cool designs on the white porcelain. I haven't done this since Mom was in the hospital. I'd forgotten how satisfying it is to experience something so completely under your own control.

"Jesus Christ." The lumberjack hovers in the door I didn't close.

"Fuck!" I drop the razor. "You scared me."

"It's a mutual feeling."

I can feel my cheeks burning as I pin him with a scowl. "Don't you have a couch to sleep on or something?"

He sighs. "I'm here for the toilet."

"Right."

I wrap a towel around my arm and disinfect the sink.

While Drew uses the bathroom, I wander to the living room and sit down beside the tree. He joins me a minute later, taking a seat across from me on the couch. He stares but doesn't say anything. His legs are crossed at the ankle and his foot twitches.

I break the silence with, "Did you leave the toilet seat up?"

I watch him poke his tongue into his cheek. He looks away and back at me.

"My wife used to do that."

I raise a brow. "Leave the seat up?"

"You're not going to make this easy, are you?"

"You know we don't have to do this. There's nothing to discuss. What did you ask Santa to bring you for Christmas?"

He closes his eyes for a moment. Draws in a deep breath.

"My wife's dead."

"Jesus. I'm sorry. I didn't realize—"

"That what happened in there is a big deal?"

"I'm starting to pick up on that, yes."

A minute passes before he can even look in my direction. I wonder what he must be thinking. Does he expect me to tell him that sometimes everything feels so unspeakably terrible that you just can't say anything? Did his wife mention that?

"You know I wasn't trying to off myself, right?"

"I don't even know what to say to that."

"How about I'm not worried anymore and let's talk about something else?"

"That's not how this works."

"What?"

"It's not your job to reassure me."

My brain can process what he's saying, but I don't know what it means. I'm busy staring at the tree and remembering how one Christmas we placed it too close to the vent and the plastic garland melted. I am that garland. Melting.

Drew looks at me expectantly, like he's waiting for me to hand over his axe.

"Was there a question?"

"What do you need?"

I roll my eyes. "You don't have to do that."

"Do what?"

"Be all supportive. You're not my guidance counsellor."

"Do you talk to your guidance counsellor?"

"Of course not."

"So why not talk to me?"

"Can't you just give me the number to a hotline or something?"

A beat passes. I'm thinking about how different my life could be if I had just closed the effin' door when he asks, "Why tonight?"

I consider his question, let if drift down softly for a moment, as if it were a feather. "How did your wife die?"

"She overdosed."

"I'm sorry. That's awful."

"Thank you. I'm sorry about your mother."

"Don't be. You're not the moose who crushed her car or the asshole who took her off life support."

"Jessie told me she was in a coma. That must have been really hard."

"David took me to the hospital every night. Dad's the one who couldn't handle it."

He nods. I've finally silenced him.

"How's your arm?"

I look down at the fresh scar. "Fine."

"Just like you?"

"I'm seventeen. What is fine supposed to be? My dad's a drunk, my mother's dead, and my brother, he's around, sometimes, but soon he won't be. How good am I supposed to feel about all that?"

"You're not. That's tough. Don't you think you should tell someone?"

"So they can feel awful, too?"

"So you can feel something else."

I turn my back to him so I can tighten one of the bulbs on the tree. It doesn't light up. Another one burns out.

"You know it won't always be this way."

I disconnect the power cord so that we're sitting in the dark. I draw in a shaky breath. "You're wrong. My mom isn't coming back. My dad isn't getting sober, and David, David will always be about David."

He gets up, takes the plug from my hand, and puts it back in the socket. "That may be true. But you forgot one person. You won't always be stuck here."

We're interrupted by Jessie storming out of my brother's room. She pulls her coat off the hook and grabs Drew's.

She whispers, "We need to go."

Drew looks at me, and I look back at him with a shrug. "Don't let me hold you up."

He looks like he's going to swear. "We're not through."

They go outside and let the truck idle. I look at the clock. It's two a.m.

Eventually my brother walks into the kitchen. No David saunter. He just paces back and forth between the counter and the coffee table in the living room. He stops there and folds his arms over his chest. "The tree looks good."

I take another look at it, trying not to think of melted garland or burnt out bulbs. "I guess."

"It's almost like she's here."

"Yeah, I miss her more when I see all this."

He goes to the kitchen and pulls out a chair. I follow him and take a seat on the counter. "You guys had a fight?"

He reaches into his shirt pocket and flips the ring on the table. "She gave it back."

Hell.

I watch him slump back in his chair; I watch him, willing to do anything to take away his pain, knowing there's no cut in my skin I could make that deep.

My father chooses that moment to walk through the back door.

"Who's truck is that out there? And what are you two doing up?"

I hop off the counter. "Oh you know, just proposing, getting dumped and cutting our wrists. The usual Christmas Eve stuff."

David stands up. "It's all good Dad. Just go to bed."

My father throws his coat over the back of a chair, shaking his head. He goes to the fridge and pulls out a six-pack of Coors then wanders down the hall muttering, "Fucking kids."

David turns to me. "Show me your arms." He looks down, then back up at me with a frown. "I thought you stopped doing that."

"I did. It was a rough night, that's all."

He stares at me, trying to decide whether or not to believe me.

"Drew walked in on me. It was really classy. He'll probably tell you all about it later."

This seems to satisfy him. We both look toward the window. The truck is still idling. We stand there together until our breath covers the glass with fog. I trace out the shape of a piece of holly with my fingertip while David turns away and lights a cigarette. He tilts his head back and blows a wreath of smoke around his face, then he drags one finger across the holly to get my attention.

"What do I do?"

I use my blood-stained sleeve to make one broad sweep across the window, erasing the fog. "Do you feel like watching *The Fast and the Furious*?"

He nods. "Yeah. I'd like that. I'd like that a lot."

The Least Interesting Thing

The thing I love most about my sister is the water pressure in her shower. You think I'm joking, but Lindsay and I haven't been close since we were kids, and I don't know who she's become as intimately as I know the settings on her shower head.

She greets me at the door with her standard mix of dismay, judgment, and anxiety. "Finally, you're here. They misspelled Adele's name on the cake and I don't have time to return it to the bakery."

Does she know we're all going to chew it up into human waste? Does she think my niece's name will be permanently misspelled inside my colon? Does she think Adele will notice? All these questions bounce inside my head as I peel off Dean's leather jacket.

She hugs me and her eyes narrow, the corners of her pinched mouth turn downwards, reminding me that I reek of sex, booze, and cigarettes. I bite down hard on the inside of my cheek instead of telling her that she smells like Listerine.

"You need a shower. There are clean towels in the basement. You've got ten minutes."

That's what I appreciate about my sister. She really takes an interest in how I'm doing.

When I step out of the shower, Adele is waiting for me, perched on the closed toilet seat in a pink tulle skirt, brandishing a star-shaped wand. "I knocked."

"But did I invite you in?"

She shrugs and asks if I know she's five today. I tell her that's why I'm here.

"To watch me turn five?"

"Yup, to watch you turn five and eat tonnes of cake."

Her shoulders slump. "You missed it, Aunt Quinn. It happened in the night, before I woke up."

I ask her if she wants me to sleep over when she turns six. She nods. "I'm sorry you missed it, Auntie Quinn. I'm sorry you're always late."

There's a moment in your life, if trauma hasn't already come along and plastered shit over everything, when it's all new. Love, the apartment, your commute, buying groceries, and paying rent. It's all precious and delicate, wrapped in tissue paper like a bra from Victoria's Secret. It's that moment before you cut the tags off and commit to the underwire, the padding, and the lace that leaves a pattern on your skin (and maybe that's new for a while, too, say three washings), and then you notice that love has funky toenails and makes a shitty roommate. The apartment is the size of a bathroom stall, your commute is a slow march towards death, culminating with your arrival in hell where you spend eternity waiting in the wrong queue at Safeway, and every day is the first of the month.

My life is past three washings. I'm thirty-one and I live with four roommates, I'm sleeping with a married man, and I'm working the front desk at a Motel Super 8 to support myself while I try to make it as a poet and spoken word artist. It's not a career path I would recommend, unless you enjoy having people stare at your shoes once you tell them what you do.

By all standards I am fucking it up. I've won the odd poetry slam, but I have over a hundred rejected poems and nothing forthcoming in any journals. I am peak fucking it up in the relationship department. The married man thing puts frost on Lindsay's ass. She doesn't understand what I see in him, and to be fair, I get it. Dean isn't a head swivelling phenomenon, but a first glance doesn't always tell the whole story. Sometimes people are attractive until they open their mouth, and then, once you've tasted the lukewarm hotdog water of their personality, the hotness evaporates. Dean is the opposite. He transforms when you hear him speak, and not just because his voice is deep. He has a dry sense of humour and a quick wit you have to pay attention to appreciate, and he doesn't talk to hear the sound of his own voice. His words are worth hanging onto.

He told me once that he could tell by the way I laughed that I'd been sad for a very long time. I suppose that's why I keep going back to him. He knows me in the most human way that we all want to be known. In the way you have to know someone if you're going to manipulate them. When you pay attention to something that's neglected, it's only natural for attachment to follow.

At six-foot three, Dean is just tall enough not to make me feel like Big Bird. As a six-foot tall woman, I spend a lot of time feeling like an oversized yellow puppet, especially when I walk on stage. On a good day, I'm a size—screw that. On a good day, I eat dessert twice and never think about what size I am. I take up space, and if you think that's brave, I can't begin to tell you what courage it takes to have brown eyes and curly hair.

When I had appendicitis, it was Dean who took me to the hospital, and when I came home after the surgery, he was the one who came to visit with minestrone soup. A year in, I know he's lying about his intentions, about wanting to leave his wife, but he also makes me feel cared for in a way that no one else does. My brother-in-law, Chris, came close once when he said, "You know he's not going to leave her for you." I nodded, and he just smiled, raising his whiskey glass. "Well then, go break your teeth."

I don't understand why people throw parties for children. As far as I'm concerned, it isn't a party until someone starts cutting lines of cocaine on the coffee table. As for birthday parties, when I was a kid, we got to choose between a box of Jos Louis or Mae Wests, and I don't see why this needs to be augmented with a bouncy castle and gifts from half the neighbourhood. I can tell all the fuss stresses Lindsay out, and I'm pretty sure Adele is just as likely to remember her mom yelling at her to keep her dress clean as she is to remember Buddy the creepy clown and his stupid balloon giraffe. I'm here because Adele wants me to be and Lindsay needs me to be. Chris is at an ill-timed legal convention in Boston. His job has its perks, but booking time off for your daughter's birthday isn't one of them.

Lindsay's kitchen is three times the size of my bedroom; I half-expect to hear an echo when I talk. It has white cabinets, granite countertops, and a farmhouse style sink. It looks like something you'd find on Pinterest, which makes sense, because Lindsay is an interior decorator and half her job is creating mood boards and browsing Pinterest. I open a drawer in search of a knife to perform surgery on the cake. Everything matches, the measuring cups and spoons, the whisk and the spatula, the soup ladle and the potato masher. They're all teal. Same as the dishes. Or is it aqua? Is there even a difference? It all says Le Creuset, and I know that's French for expensive as fuck.

I feel bad for hating her house so much. It's just such a far cry from the way we came up, mopping our dishes clean with rags cut from worn out T-shirts. Sure, I'm jealous, because I know it isn't going to happen for me (or that I won't let it?) but I really want to ask if she's happier in her modern, colour-coordinated kitchen, or if she ever misses opening a can of Spam, slicing it on a diagonal, slathering it in mustard, microwaving it for two minutes, and devouring it on a piece of white toast. Does she ever take a can of tomato juice and reheat it with elbow macaroni on a rainy afternoon, the way our mom did for us, or has she hosted too many cocktail parties to remember how to prepare peasant food with a can opener? Does she even own one? A teal can opener?

I guess that's what happens when you marry a corporate lawyer. You move up. Away from the hood, into the suburbs, so you can raise your kids away from all the condoms and needles and broken glass on the sidewalk. Feed them fresh and organic, keep them so precious they won't even need tetanus shots.

The theme of the party is *Frozen*. I haven't seen the entire film, but I've seen parts of it repeatedly, so I know that Sven and Olaf are the comic relief, and I understand why Lindsay sings, "Turn it off, turn it off," to the tune of "Let It Go." The kids play musical chairs, pin the carrot on Olaf, and smack a Sven-shaped piñata. This is followed by gifts and cake. My job is to take pictures, which is the perfect excuse not to engage with the other adults who invariably start the conversation with "Which one is yours?" or my favourite, "When are you due?"

Partway through the afternoon Dean texts me to say I left my underwear in the backseat of his car. When I look up from my phone, Lindsay is staring at me, her lip curled in disgust.

The whole day is a yawn until I run upstairs to Lindsay's bathroom for some Tylenol. I can hear her retching. It's the soundtrack of my childhood, so this isn't exactly a shock. Lindsay looks like a Calvin Klein model from the nineties, updated with micro-bladed eyebrows.

The first time I caught Lindsay purging, she was fifteen and we were in a bathroom at McDonald's. She slammed me into the side of the stall and made me swear not to tell our mother. It was the last promise I made to her. I was eleven.

I raise my hand to knock on the door and ask if she's okay, but when I open my mouth to speak nothing comes out and my hand falls to my side. I know she's not okay, and I know she'll tell me she's *fine*, the way she has probably been telling Chris for months, and on and off again for years. She went into treatment at one point, and she was doing well until Adele was born.

I forget about the Tylenol and go back to the party. I hand out loot bags and thank people for coming. Adele falls asleep on the couch within minutes and I carry her up to her room. Lindsay and I clean up the kitchen in silence. I'm hauling the Hefty bag filled with plastic forks and paper plates to the back door when I spin around and blurt, "How many times a day?"

Her eyes widen for a half a second before she lowers them and I'm sure she's going to bullshit me. Her shoulders slump a little. "Two, sometimes three."

"Jesus."

"I need you to stay with Adele."

"For the night?"

"No. I need you to stay with her while I'm in treatment."

This is big. The last time was a couple years before Adele was born. "What makes you think Chris can't handle it?"

She wanders to the living room and sinks into the couch. It's leather and it makes a farting noise as she slides back into the cushions. "He's having an affair."

This, too, is not entirely shocking.

"I see."

"I don't want him bringing her here. I don't want Adele to find out. I really need you to do this for me."

I grew up listening to my sister vomiting as discretely as anyone could. I want Adele to hear a different lullaby.

"I'll have to ask for time from work."

"Like Dean won't grant you any favours."

Even when she's asking for my help, she's judging me. "Do you know who she is?"

"His personal trainer."

No wonder she's puking. How did we get so far from reheated Spam? My-husband-is sleeping-with-his-personal-trainer isn't a problem working-class people tend to have. "Does he know that you know?"

"He's the one who told me."

"So it's over?" She gives me a withering look that reminds me of a time when she could make me cry with one cutting glance.

"Hardly."

Who confesses to an affair without promising to break it off? For a minute, I want to choke this trainer with her own resistance bands, and then I remember who I am, and that in different ways, we are each being used. Chris is the one who has it all.

"I don't even know why I'm telling you this."

I'm about to reply that I don't know either when Adele appears. Her eyes are still heavy from sleep. She climbs on the couch between us and turns on the television. From the menu, she selects a movie, and of course, it's *Frozen*. Lindsay goes upstairs to soak in the tub, and I resign myself to the cartoon. It resonates more than I'd like it to—sisterhood and shit—but the princesses make me want to tear my eyelashes out, one by one. They're all the same from one film to the next. Bouncy hair, tiny bodies, and eyes that take up half their faces. When I was Adele's age, I was obsessed with the Little Mermaid, but eventually I became aware that the only person built like me was Ursula, the sea witch. It was my first lesson in fat equals villain. I need to introduce Adele to Mulan.

After the movie and a peanut butter sandwich, Adele asks me to tuck her into bed. Apparently my sister told her tomorrow comes faster when you go to bed early, and she's excited for tomorrow because Daddy gets home from his trip, and she gets to celebrate her birthday again with him. I'm lying on the twin mattress next to her. She has her *Frozen* comforter pulled up to her chin, and I'm almost certain she's asleep when she says, "I think I ate too much cake."

"Aw. Does your stomach hurt?"

"No, I'm scared I'll get fat."

I'd sacrifice my front teeth to a hockey puck to never hear those words from my five-year-old niece.

"You don't want to be like me?"

"I'd rather be like Mom."

Married to a cheat, purging three times a day, driving alone for eight hours to a private clinic that charges twenty grand?

I turn on the lamp.

"I wanted to be like your mom when I was little, too." She gives me a look, as if to ask what happened. "But I turned out like me, and you're going to be you, and whoever that is, whatever she looks like, it's fine." She doesn't seem persuaded. The Disney princess damage has already been done. "Look, there are two things I need you to remember: First, how you look is the least interesting thing about you, and second, food is part of how we say yes to life."

She scrunches up her face. "What does that mean?"

"It means when you're old, I don't want you to remember going to bed hungry. I want you to remember eating cake. You'll understand later."

"When I'm six?"

"Maybe seven."

"Aunt Quinn?"

"Yeah?"

"What's the most interesting thing about me?"

My phone vibrates. It's Dean. I was supposed to meet him tonight. I let it go to voicemail, turn to Adele, and drop a kiss on her forehead. "Your imagination."

Blind Date

I did it because I wanted to throw back a few glasses of merlot, and the thought of having a meal with it was a nice touch compared to the ramen noodles waiting for me at home. It was a Thursday, the first week of the month, and I was waiting on my direct deposit to buy groceries.

My brother worked at Lina's, this Italian Bistro. They really knew their gnocchi, and they were classy, even if they were crowded. The seating was Tony's pet peeve. Like pull your chair in already, will you? I guess it was a nice place if you were trying to impress someone and you liked garlic bread.

I came to drop off the car keys. I needed the Neon for an interview and some errands that day, and while Tony didn't mind taking the bus to work, he hated taking it home.

I waited for Tony near the bar, trying not to be in anyone's way while I studied the half-litre of house red on the table nearest me and listened to my stomach growl. I had lunched on two watermelon Starburst fruit chews. The white damask napkins were contorted into origami swans, and the man at the table with the wine looked equally uncomfortable. He kept checking his watch; it was a little endearing that he was wearing one. It might have been a status symbol, but I couldn't tell a Timex from a Rolex.

"Blind date," Tony whispered, leaning against the bar beside me. "And he's totally getting stood up."

I looked at his crisp pinstripe shirt, probably freshly starched and pressed from the cleaner's, and tried to summon some empathy. My stomach growled again. I'm not sure it's possible to feel empathy when you're hungry. It's one of those gentrified emotions reserved for people who already have their needs met. "How long has he been waiting?"

Tony shrugged. "Twenty-five minutes. At least."

"Someone should put him out of his misery."

"Yeah."

I was at the table in three strides.

"Sorry I'm late."

He looked up, relieved. His smile faded a little. "Weren't you just at the bar?"

My face reddened as I dropped my coat over the back of the chair. "It's so embarrassing. I was having trouble finding you."

"Didn't you give my name to the hostess?"

I sat down and reached for the wine. "Oh she was no help. That waiter," I waved at Tony, "helped me find you."

He turned to look at Tony, giving him a nod, and I was satisfied that he was satisfied. I rewarded myself by gulping down half the glass of wine.

* * *

The thing about losing your job is that you lose all your confidence, which is pretty sad because it's all I had left. I didn't even get to take a cardboard file box with my personal effects because I was a proofreader with a touchdown space. I just left with my messenger bag, like any other day. I spent the next two days watching the Women's Network, coiled in a pit of blankets on the couch, fortifying myself with cartons of chow mein, ginger beef, and spring rolls. When I finally showered, I realized something extra had washed down the drain. I couldn't place what was missing until I phoned my brother to ask if I could crash on his couch, so I could sublet the apartment. He asked if I would be okay, and the thing I needed to reassure him wasn't there. I didn't know, and I didn't like it. It was my job to know shit, except now, I didn't have a job. I missed my confidence each time I wrote a cover letter and sent out my resume, and also before grocery shopping because I was afraid to check my account balance. I winced each time I punched my PIN into the debit machine.

One day I was an adult and the next I was just a kid, afraid of her own shadow. For the first time in my twenty-eight years, I understood why people bought self-help books: losing your confidence is a bitch. It was like I forgot what shelf I put it on. Scratch that. I knew exactly what shelf it was on and it was just too high to reach. So there I was, jumping, arms in the air, snatching at it, and feeling more stupid by the minute. I was doing all the things women are taught to do to cheer themselves up: buying lipstick in a bold shade you'll never wear so you can tell yourself you're being adventurous, soaking in a hot bath until your eczema burns so you can say you practise self-care, going to the movies alone, to show you're independent. Learning to knit, creative, until your dish cloth looks like a loin cloth because you've dropped so many stitches. And yoga, because people who exercise think they're better than everyone else.

My date, as I decided to think of him, watched me from narrowed eyes as I refilled my glass. He was no hardship to look at. From chin to nose he had a Michael Fassbender thing going on: the gleaming, shark-toothed smile, equal parts attractive and predatory. A jawline sharper than the knives in my kitchen, and a well-trimmed goatee with one tiny patch where the hair didn't grow, likely from a scar. He had green eyes and a fringe of sooty lashes that could have sold a lot of mascara for Maybelline. Clearly, I wasn't in the habit of sitting across from men who looked like celebrities.

"How was your day?"

I thought about my interview with *Fast Forward Weekly*, and how I had taken my fourteen-year-old cat to the vet to be euthanized, earlier in the morning. I tried not to think about what I was doing at this table. "Still young. Too early to tell." He seemed to like that answer. It un-furrowed his brow. "How was yours?"

"Pretty tame. So far." He winked, and I was almost as worried as I was hungry and faint. I'd had a cup of coffee in the morning, and not a drop of liquid had passed my lips since. I was certain I'd cried at least six ounces of tears between the vet and the interview. The wine was hitting me hard.

"Do you know what you're having?" I didn't know how far I could take this, but if I could manage it, I was going all the way to dessert.

"I haven't finished looking at the menu."

Great. He was one of those. The kind who read the entire menu twice before they place an order.

He was frowning again. "Did you dye your hair?"

Oh, no. "You know most women prefer not to be asked about that." Nothing beats two glasses of red on an empty stomach to restore your confidence.

"Sorry, it's just that Jimmy said you were a brunette."

"I like to switch things up."

"Well, it looks natural. Red suits you."

"It's auburn, and I'll pass the compliment to my stylist."

Tony delivered a bread basket and drizzled a plate with oil. He told us to enjoy, and then he turned to me and mouthed, *I hope you choke.*

"I need a cigarette."

"I didn't realize—"

"Let me guess, Jimmy said I don't."

"Uh, yeah."

"I'm off the wagon. It only happens when I get nervous."

I reached for the pack of Peter Jacksons (oh, the pain of small economies) in my purse and slid one out, leaving two behind. My date arched a brow.

"You must be really nervous."

I poked my tongue into my cheek, searching for a reply. "Don't tell," the wine leaned in and whispered for me. I made sure to push in my chair all the way when I got up. "If the waiter comes to take our order, tell him I'll have the gnocchi."

As soon as I stepped into the alley, I wished I'd brought my coat. The chinook that had devoured most of the snow was turning cold. March and April were the most vindictive months in Calgary.

I fumbled with my lighter. The fluid was almost drained and the gusting wind didn't help. I watched a flattened paper Tim Hortons cup dance past me, Canadian Beauty style. Finally, I struck a light.

Tony appeared at my shoulder. "You know there's a word for taking something that isn't yours. It's called stealing."

This was a lot coming from my brother. He was fundamentally immune to what others thought, like people who give out pencils on Halloween. I wasn't in the mood for his sudden development of a conscience.

"Was it stealing when I brought Sylvester in from the rain?"

"He didn't belong to anyone."

"And this guy does?"

"Just because his date abandoned him doesn't give you license to mess with his head."

I took a drag on my cigarette. "Maybe I'm serious."

"Just get in there and fix it before I have to serve you again."

I came back to the table feeling chilled and smelling like an ashtray.

"So Jennifer, what do you do for fun?"

Fun? Wasn't that something that happened accidentally as you hurried from one job to the next? Did people actually slow down without hearing the background noise of their worries, humming like the refrigerator? Did he mean how I relaxed? Because I couldn't imagine doing that without a cat purring on my chest.

I took a piece of bread and dragged it through the oil. "Call me Jen."

"Alright, Jen. What do you do for fun?"

"You mean apart from drinking, smoking, and going on blind dates?"

One corner of his mouth lifted into a smile. "Jimmy didn't tell me you were so glamorous."

Nothing says glamorous like a white poplin blouse from H&M and black micro-twill pants peppered with ginger cat hair. It was pathetic. Not just because I was evidently below his standards, but because this was me trying to impress a potential employer. I didn't even brush off the cat hair because it was all of Sylvester I had left.

"Words must have failed him." I bit down on my piece of bread. "What do you do for fun?"

"I play baseball, and I like to fish. I go out to Kananaskis every chance I get."

"Catch and release?" It sounded like I knew something, but really, I'd just seen the film.

"Nah. Clean and fry. Have you ever had fresh pan-fried trout?"

I took another bite of bread. "Jimmy didn't tell you?"

"Glaring oversight. Have you?"

"Not that I can remember."

"You'd remember."

"Speaking of remembering, do you think they forgot our order?"

He looked at his watch. "It's barely been ten minutes."

"Feels longer. I must be hungry."

His gaze wandered to the bread basket. "Apparently."

Wanting to change the subject I said, "Tell me about your work."

Our food arrived at the same moment he told me he was in family law. So he was intelligent. Ambitious. Confident. Fuck me. He talked briefly about his practice before asking,

"What's your job like?"

I wanted to say that I'd spent four years in J-school preparing to stock shelves at the Shawnessy Walmart Super-centre because media convergence had butt-fucked me like an elephant, but not all roads lead to flourless chocolate cake. "I have a strict policy about not talking shop after hours."

"C'mon. I understand client privilege, but at least tell me something. Like how you got started."

Oh Jesus. I was supposed to have clients? I looked down at the steam rolling off my plate. "I just wanted to help people, you know?"

"Mmm. And do you enjoy it? Helping people?"

"You sound like a lawyer."

"Do I? How's that?"

"You seem suspicious."

"Well, isn't helping people a vague notion? It could have led you to be a teacher or a nurse."

"Jimmy didn't tell you I spent a year in nursing school?"

"Jimmy forgot a lot of things."

"Such as?"

"That you have a cat."

Had. "You don't like felines?"

"Extremely allergic."

"I guess we're not going back to my apartment."

"And he forgot to mention your sense of humour."

"Not everyone appreciates it."

"How's your food?"

"Hot."

There was a lull in our conversation while I attacked the gnocchi as efficiently as possible, without completely burning my mouth. I could tell he was studying me, but I didn't care, as long as it didn't interfere with my chewing.

Eventually he said, "How long has it been?"

"Since?"

"Your husband passed."

Tony almost got his wish. I reached for the wine, took three gulps, and cleared my throat. "It's uh, fairly recent."

"I'm terribly sorry."

That made two of us. Maybe I could make my emergency exit to the bathroom. Would he think it strange if I took my coat?

He set his napkin on the table. A blob of tomato sauce stained the white damask, reminding me of who I was.

"Will you excuse me for a moment?"

"Of course." I noticed he pushed the chair in all the way.

He paused and turned back to me. "If the waiter comes by with the dessert menu, let him know I'll have the cheesecake."

Tony appeared a moment later. "Having fun?"

"I know. There's a special place in hell. He'll have the cheesecake by the way."

Dessert came faster than my date's return, and I stared at it for a full five minutes before I was sure of what was happening. This was what it was like to get played. I felt like the kid at Disneyland who had just seen Mickey take his head off to light up a cigarette. Tony came back for no better reason than to ask how I was enjoying the first few bites.

"He's gone, isn't he?"

"Oh yeah."

"What's the damage?"

"More than you can afford."

Damn you, Michael Lawyer Fassbender.

"I'm gonna need this table. Why don't you wait at the bar, until that deposit of yours kicks in?"

I spent the next two hours sipping a glass of water and picking individual cat hairs off my pants. I should have known he saw through me the minute he told me he was a lawyer. Mercifully, my deposit was in by ten forty-five. I waved Tony down for the debit machine, but he came back with the car keys instead.

"Go home. I'll get a ride."

"What about the bill?"

"Romeo paid it."

"You let me sit here for two hours—"

"Hey, not everyone believes in rewarding bad behaviour."

"Wait, did he say anything?"

"Like what? Thanks for playing?"

"His name maybe. Did he pay with a credit card? Do you have the slip?"

Tony grinned. He held the receipt over my head, just beyond my fingertips. I jumped, and this time I could reach.

Coke, No Contest

I dreamed about him all the time, dreamed that we were in school together and that our teachers were endlessly separating us. Owen and I weren't friends and he'd never been a crush. We had the tenuous small-town connection of having parents who were acquainted with each other, if only tragically.

When I was six, I discovered an envelope of photographs shoved in the back of the silverware drawer in our china cabinet. Inside I found a collection of snapshots of a long-haired pirate with the same almond-shaped eyes and cut-from-glass dimples as my mother. Okay, he wasn't a pirate, but he had a Long John Silver thing happening. He rocked a moustache the way George Harrison wished he could, and bell-bottoms the way an entire generation would collectively regret. Nearly every picture featured him holding an acoustic guitar and a cigarette, except for the ones where he had his arm draped around a pretty redhead.

I didn't tell anyone about this discovery, not even my sister, but I returned to the envelope when I needed to escape to somewhere else in my mind. I created an entire universe for these people I didn't know, full of pirates and swords.

Eventually I learned that in addition to her younger twin brothers, my mother had an older brother who died by suicide in 1969. He'd shot himself in the head, and the woman who found him, his pretty redhead girlfriend, later became Owen's mother. There was a six-page police report and an unspeakable sadness linking our families. Our skeletons shared a closet.

My mother processed most of the grief through her liver. She'd been a happy-go-lucky eighteen-year-old when it happened, and she responded by adopting a fatalism that only the devil could reckon with. She never said no to a dare or a drink, or any substance. By the time I was old enough to pay attention, chardonnay was her poison of choice, and she killed at least two bottles every night. It's hard to say exactly what killed her. She had a stroke at fifty-six, and was expected to make a full recovery, but she died a few weeks later. Her heart just stopped. It had certainly been broken for long enough.

With my mother dead for three years and my last year of high school over fifteen years behind me, I didn't have much reason to dream about Owen. I couldn't remember the last time we'd seen each other or spoken, and it annoyed me tremendously that I kept thinking of him, but I couldn't summon a dream for the many people I had once cared for instead.

They weren't bad dreams either, not like the ones I had about university or drowning in the Highwood River off the Canadian Pacific Railway bridge. The drowning one I'd been having since I was five, and it made an appearance every few years, just often enough to remind me of how small and helpless we all are. The university dream was a graduation gift. I had six more science credits (the impossible!) to complete. I didn't finish my undergrad until I was thirty, and the whole time I thought those six credits would end me. Clearly, it was a mistake to enrol in astronomy, but it was a curious dream to keep having now that I was finally teaching. It was as if I imagined my degree could be revoked, some sort of imposter syndrome where my students and the entire faculty discover I've brought the blue collar and all its associated diseases into the ivory tower.

My dreams about Owen happened more often, and they were more confusing. With the bridge I knew I was going to drown and with university I knew I was going to fail, but with him I could never quite remember what went on. We were in school, but the rest was a little hazy. Our teachers tried to keep us apart, but we had never spent any amount of time together. He sat behind me in English one year, and that was the peak of our proximity.

"That's creepy," my sister said when I finished telling her over Sunday brunch. It was my week to host, and I'd gone all out and served bacon with eggs and French toast. We were sitting in my improvised breakfast nook at a table I had rescued from the dumpster. It was the perfect size and I didn't mind that it was badly scratched. Amidst all the curses a heart was etched into one corner. It read Suzy + Dan = forever. It would have been a shame to let such love decompose on a garbage heap, so I brought it home and covered it with a lace tablecloth so the graffiti and their eternal commitment could breathe.

I rolled my eyes at Angie. "I know. I'm the worst."

"No, I mean, it's spooky."

"How so?"

"He's in a coma." She poured herself some juice. "Aren't you on Facebook?"

"You know I am. You created my profile. What happened?"

"Apparently there was a car accident."

I put my coffee cup back in its saucer. "Was anyone else hurt?"

"He was alone."

"You mean there wasn't another vehicle?"

"No. He crashed into a concrete overpass."

"Shit. That's awful."

"Awfully suspicious." She flipped her hair over her shoulder in a way so familiar, so like our mother that it made me queasy. "They say alcohol wasn't a factor. You'd think he tried."

"Don't say things like that. Someone might repeat it."

"Too late. Everyone's saying it already."

I used my fork to push the last bite of toast around on my plate. "Doesn't he have a wife and kids?"

"Yeah, why?"

"Well maybe they don't need to hear that shit."

"What if it's the truth?"

I stood up and scraped the toast and some egg yolk off my plate and into the garbage. "The truth is overrated."

Angie dropped her elbows on the table and rested her cheeks in the palms of her hands. "So what does Niall have to say about all this?"

Niall was my boyfriend, and he lived with me when he wasn't travelling, which was often. He worked on a film crew and he was away on shoots more than he was home, but I didn't mind because he was emphatically *safe*. He had three older sisters, and somehow that had taught him to see women as people, as well as how to braid hair. He did a remarkable job with the French braid for my sister's wedding.

* * *

To tell the truth, the dreams were kind of bittersweet. I woke up calm and peaceful, and all I could figure, if I had to analyze it, was that I missed being a kid. Didn't everyone long for the innocence now and then? Why Owen happened to be my dreamscape companion didn't seem important because he didn't ruin anything, and I didn't care how often I had the dreams because they were pleasant. I always felt safe, and the teachers who tried to separate us never succeeded. Nothing could break us apart, and that was fine, until I learned he was in a coma. Then understanding my dreams became of paramount importance.

The possibility of a collective unconscious that warehoused shared memories and trauma had always seemed doubtful to me. Since it wasn't logical or measurable, I dismissed it onto a pile of theories I called total horse shit. The pile was mainly composed of Freud and old-wives tales passed down from my mother, like needing to wait an hour after you eat to go swimming. There was just a dash of Jung for good measure.

I wasn't expecting to have the dream again, now that I knew about the accident, but a week later I woke up at four a.m., half sure I was still eleven, and of course Owen was with me.

Why couldn't I just dream about my teeth falling out like everyone else?

* * *

"So I asked Google what it means when you keep dreaming about the same person." It was Angie's turn to host and we were drinking mimosas on her balcony.

I groaned. "This should be good."

"Turns out it's all about unresolved stuff," she said stirring her drink. "Like if you keep dreaming about the same ex, you're probably dealing with the same issues in your current relationship."

"Now that sounds like a direct quote from a peer-reviewed journal."

"Don't be such a snob."

I sighed. "Owen is not my ex. He wasn't even my friend, and there's nothing unresolved between us."

Her eyes narrowed. "Didn't he ask you out in like seventh grade?"

"It was sixth, and how did you remember that?"

"Why'd you shoot him down? He was the best-looking ginger in school."

"Was he a ginger though? I thought he was more of a daywalker."

"Pretty sure this happened before South Park gifted us that term."

Owen resembled his mother, minus the celestial nose. He had the same deep set, blue-grey eyes and a jawline made for a Gillette Mach 3 commercial. It was a little hard to imagine what he saw in me, buried in lumberjack shirts and hiding behind wire-framed glasses. Back then, all the girls were stumbling around in platform shoes and baby tees. I was the only one who didn't smell like Love's Baby Soft perfume and watermelon Lip Smackers. I was the girl stuck on Hole and Nirvana in the era of Backstreet Boys and Britney Spears.

Angie tapped a nail against her glass. "Well, why did you say no? He wasn't an asshole like all those boys grabbing our asses and snapping our bra straps."

I smiled. "He was nice. But if I'd said yes, he would have wanted to break up with me in two weeks."

"You think he would have given you the full fourteen days?"

"Fine. Four. Whatever. You know what I mean."

"So you liked him?"

I paused to drain my glass. "No. Worse. I respected him."

"How is that worse?"

"I was too distracted by the assholes snapping my bra straps to realize it."

"So there's your unresolved conflict."

I shrugged and held out the glass for a refill. "Google solved it."

* * *

I have a profound understanding of what students are meant to take away from high school English because I teach an ELA-30 upgrading course and Introductory Composition. I expect my students to come to me knowing certain things, but they rarely do. I'm disappointed, if not surprised. But I shouldn't be. When I think about what I retained from my own experience, it wasn't fanboys or transitive and intransitive verbs. Much to the chagrin of my teachers, I consistently misspelled separate, and I used American endings for words like colour and odour. I devoured *The Outsiders* and was blown away by how young S.E. Hinton was when she wrote it. Then we watched the film in class and I decided it spoiled the entire experience. There are some things even Patrick Swayze can't save.

I remember how Mr. Graves leaned against the chalkboard, acquiring a white stripe across the seat of his navy trousers, earning him the nickname Chalk-Ass. I remember trying to read *The Taming of the Shrew* and my sister renting me a VHS copy from Blockbuster. I turned in the first of many papers about a book I didn't finish. I remember cutting class to get stoned beside the dumpster that said *Fuck Ralph Klein* in fluorescent pink paint the fresh coat of green couldn't quite cover and making out with Josh Hendricks beside it. I remember walking into the boy's washroom on my first day of ninth grade and wondering when they installed the urinals before staring directly into the eyes of a goth dude coming out of a stall.

And I remember clearly how one day we hijacked the conversation about advertising and media literacy and turned it into a debate about which was the superior beverage, Pepsi or Coke. I remember a voice behind me muttering, "Coke, no contest."

At the time I hardly drank soft drinks, but with a little experience I can say it was the right answer. I wouldn't waste my rum on Pepsi.

Was it the brand loyalty that made an impression on me? Or just the absolute certainty? How did I forget the periodic table and retain *Coke, no contest*? And perhaps more importantly, how could that be the only thing I knew about someone I went to school with for twelve years?

But it was the only thing I knew about Owen, and feeling like I should do something to honour him, I purchased a six pack of votives and a can of Coke at the dollar store, and I cleared a space for them next to the stack of books on my bedside table. I lit the candle and let the Coke sweat and grow warm, unopened. I said what religious people might have called a prayer. I kept up the routine for a week.

When Niall finally came home, he inquired about the installation. I told him it was an experiment.

He frowned. "What's the hypothesis?"

I answered him by asking if he preferred Pepsi or Coke.

He thought for a minute. "I like root beer."

* * *

I made a shepherd's pie for Angie just so I would have an excuse to drop by her apartment and ask, "Do you know what happened to that envelope of pictures of Uncle Jeremy?"

"It must be in a box somewhere in the spare room. Why?"

"How old were you when you found out about him?"

Angie scrunched up her face. "Seven, maybe eight. I was with Mom at the Spruce Meadows Christmas Market, and we ran into Owen's mother and they stopped to talk. Afterward, I asked who she was and Mom said she used to date your uncle. I asked if it was Sean or Pat, and she said no, your uncle Jeremy."

"She actually said his name?"

"Yeah, but she refused to answer my questions, so I asked Uncle Pat and he gave me the Fisher-Price Coles notes."

"What did that sound like?"

"Oh, I don't know. Our older brother died when he was young and your mom doesn't like to talk about it because it makes her very sad, so don't ask. Then he told me about how Jeremy and his girlfriend would take him and Sean to the movies. He said she had a really great voice and that she and Jeremy would sing 'Bobby McGee' all the time in the car."

It was easier to think about pirates and treasure than to wonder what happens to young love prematurely terminated by death. Break ups were hard enough. Maybe that's why I couldn't forget Owen. I didn't know him and I still knew way too much. And how much did he know? Was his mother more open than ours? Who sits their kid down to say this super traumatic thing happened to me when I was seventeen? But why shouldn't Owen have had an uncle Pat to feed him the Fisher-Price Coles version: Your mom's first boyfriend died "unexpectedly." She found his body. That's why she doesn't sing anymore. By the way, you go to school with his nieces. Not likely. Who would say that to a kid? No wonder my mother didn't discuss it.

I did a few of my own Google searches about dreams. I tried picking up Jung's *Psychology of the Unconscious*, which I quickly exchanged for a copy of *Jane Eyre*. I'm not sure why I chose it because I liked Austen better than all the Brontës combined, but it was very much a book I wasn't finished with, even though I'd read all of it. It hinged on the idea that we had souls that could be eternally damned and that we weren't just empty vessels escorting each other through life. I didn't accept Jane's reason for leaving Rochester, and if she really forgave him, on the spot, as she said, she would have acted accordingly. It seemed like an avoidable tragedy. I kept coming back to the part where she said it was her spirit addressing his, as if they'd passed through the grave and stood at God's feet. Why didn't he tell her she wouldn't pass through it, that it was where she would stay and rot? He must have loved her. And maybe that was the part that pissed me off. I don't think he would have left her for anything. Certainly not the mere promise of an afterlife.

The next time I saw Angie, she told me Owen was dead.

"I know. I had another dream."

Her eyebrows shot up. "What happened?"

"I was waiting for him on the bleachers on the soccer field and he never came. I fell asleep."

"That was it?"

"That was it." I didn't tell her about the kiss.

I'm not sure why I lied and told her it was a soccer field. It was a basketball court and he was playing one-on-one with my dead uncle. I think I was meant to be keeping score, but I fell asleep and when I woke up it was dark in the gymnasium. He was beside me and he took my hand and he led me out, past all of the boys who taunted and groped me, and we went back to the playground and sat on the swings.

When I opened my eyes, daylight had just begun to spill over the horizon. I brought the can of warm Coke with me to the kitchen and poured it into two glasses and downed them both. I sat down at my rescue table and peeled back the lace on the corner where the heart was etched. Tracing my finger over it, I wondered how eternity was working out for Suzy and Dan, if they had upgraded their table to solid oak, or if they had slowly forgotten each other the way I had forgotten the meaning of all those symbols in the periodic table.

I took my copy of *Jane Eyre,* tore a page out and crumpled it in my fist. The sound of the paper rustling against itself was like music. I tore out another and another until I was left holding a spine joining two covers. I sat down in the middle of the scattered pages and shuffled the pile with my feet. I made a paper fan and a fleet of airplanes that I sent flying around the room. I lay back and pretended to make a snow angel. Then I got up and threw away the whole mess. Or I thought I did. I found a page under the couch when I was moving out of the apartment. It was the one when Jane hears Rochester calling her name.

The Fault Is Yours

This was in the year of *fuck it, I'm going to live*, and it was working out badly. If you're not familiar, *fuck it, I'm going to live* is a diet, a budget, and a beauty regimen. It's calorie dense, high interest, and retinol based. It's *Eat, Pray, Love* for people who are afraid to fly or can't afford a plane ticket. People like me, who have anxiety attacks every time they walk to the mailbox.

If I had to give a status update, I'd say the fuck it part is going well, especially if you count fucking up in addition to surrendering, and the living part is a bit of a disappointment. Like I'm breathing, but kinda shallow and sometimes I have to concentrate. If living means buying random vintage turquoise and La Mer face cream, I've nailed it. If it means showering every day and leaving the house more than once a week, I may have some progress to make.

I always thought if my husband left me, it would be for another woman, someone leggy and coltish, with freckles on her nose and no bags under her eyes. Instead, I got the shaft for an unborn child who doesn't even exist yet. I feel more cheated than if he had committed adultery. I'd love to have an attractive, younger woman to direct my anger at. I want a perfectly symmetrical face I can tape over the bull's-eye and sink my darts into. I want to be jealous. Of the crown of hair on her head and the places on her temples where it hasn't started to recede. I want to be jealous of her voice, her laugh, the croissant she ate for breakfast and her thigh gap. But all I can picture is the blurry photo you get to take home after the ultrasound that confirms the baby has a heartbeat.

Enter online shopping. While Sam packs up his portion of the decade we spent together as we continue to live under the same roof, I fill my cart with Pottery Barn Kids items for an over-priced nursery we'll never have. Don't be fooled. Mine is not the story of repeated miscarriages, many rounds of failed IVF, or yards of adoption red tape. Sam isn't leaving because I can't have a baby. He's leaving because I won't.

When I was fifteen, I stopped sleeping regularly. One or two hours a night was all I needed, and in the time I should have spent sleeping, I began painting a series of self-portraits inspired by Frida Kahlo because I wanted to create an entire universe, and I felt so important I didn't question putting myself at the centre of it. My appetite disappeared along with my need for sleep; I shrank proportionally as my collection of canvasses grew. For the first time in my life I was thin. And chatty. Small talk never came easily, but now my friends told me to shut up. After six weeks of vibrating with this new energy and wit, I crashed. I started sleeping twelve hours a night, and the frenzied brush strokes came to a halt. The voices, and suddenly I realized that it was voices that had compelled me to paint, were gone, and I was left a shell of a person with a half-finished project. I hit a shallow, white working-class rock bottom. My family doctor prescribed Paxil, and when I failed to improve and became actively suicidal, she increased the dose. After my mother discovered me crying in a ball under the coffee table, she decided it might be worth getting a second opinion, which led to a hospital and a cesspool of conflicting diagnoses. I began a cycle of rinse, lather, repeat with a range of antidepressants.

Five years later, some bright fucker finally decided that I had bipolar disorder, which meant that all the antidepressants I had been taking were aggravating my condition. I was part of the mentally-ill elite who sought help and actually got it (trust me, we are as rare and fabled as unicorns), and somehow I still got screwed over. I'd be lying if I said it didn't change me. My expectations for myself and the world around me calcified. I took my meds as prescribed and washed them down with bourbon. I kept my paintings, not because I intended to finish them, but because I needed a reminder. I gave the series a title: A Place I Never Want to Go Again. When I'm feeling low, I pull them out. They're awful oils with heavy brush strokes, and it helps. At least it did, until now, which is why I have onesies, a mobile, and a muslin swaddle set in my shopping cart.

We have all these rituals surrounding weddings, but at least there's this compass to point you in the right direction. You wear a white dress, Dad walks you down the aisle, vows, rings, kiss. Divorce is shrouded in mystery and legalese. It's like going ass over tea kettle down a staircase. Yeah, I'm grateful there isn't a crowd of people waiting for me at the bottom, but I also wish there was just one person to help me up. For the last ten years, that person has been my husband.

Sam is considerate, which is why he waited until July, when I'm not teaching, to tell me that he can't do this anymore, that he needs a deeper sense of purpose, that he wanted to have children so he could leave a legacy. What we had, which included time to sleep in, have sex, and linger over books and coffee, was no longer enough. He felt like his life was pointless without children, and I didn't have the heart to ask, what if it's pointless with them?

We didn't rush into our marriage without discussing my stance on kids. We agreed, and we celebrated by adopting a rescue dog, a mid-life, overlooked beagle mix named Bowie who took up more than his fair share of the bed and loved nothing more than licking mashed banana and peanut butter from his Kong. He continuously demanded refills by dropping it at my feet. Lately it makes my heart burst to know I could make Bowie so completely happy. Without sacrifice. I don't hate babies or the notion of motherhood. I'm just not willing to take a hellcation from mood stabilizers and antipsychotics in order to conceive. It would be feasible for me to try that and have it turn out so badly that it, too, would decimate my marriage, and possibly my career.

Or maybe our marriage was doomed from the start because I chose a psychiatric nurse. Sam picks up on things other people miss, like when I lose interest in food and hobbies. From day one he could recognize a depressive episode on the horizon, but it took him longer to get a grasp on the hypomanic stuff. The gleam in my eye and the easy laughter didn't set off alarm bells the way skipping showers and not vacuuming the carpet did. He says I even chew my food differently when I'm depressed. "It's like watching you push sawdust around in your mouth."

Sometimes I wonder if he fell in love with a version of me that doesn't actually exist. Certainly some of his best memories of us are braided into the hypomanic episodes. I don't zip-line or climb rock walls when I'm stable. I like my feet on the ground, or better yet, a chair under my bottom. Sam is always telling me I need to be more active, that it's the best way to prevent a depressive episode, but my level of activity is also a reliable indicator of a hypomanic one.

The biggest argument of our marriage happened six months ago, and it was over me not wanting to run a half-marathon. "We don't do anything together. It would be good for us. Especially you."

I didn't know whether to lose my shit over the first part or the last. We cooked and ate supper together every night. Watched hockey side by side all season. What he meant is that we didn't climb mountains or race go-carts. Axe throwing was the most adventurous thing I'd done in years. *Especially me* meant I needed to do something about the weight gain from the antipsychotic. The new one he recommended I try. I told him he could take Abilify for eight months and see if his ass still fit in his pants, which unleashed a storm of *always* and *nevers* hurled against me. I always blamed him for my difficulties, I never wanted to try new things, I always did what suited me, and I never considered what he wanted. The implication was that what he wanted was better for my health, and I said as much.

Things changed after that. Sam withdrew his support from my network. He no longer asked about my appointments or my mood. He elected to stop dealing with my illness, and if I could make that decision, I would too.

Sam wasn't *my* nurse, not him with all the power and me with all the unmet needs, a ripe manic-pixie-dream-peach, ready to be picked by a hero complex. We met because I was speaking about my lived experience on a panel he attended. I'd been approached by my psychiatrist because she knew I volunteered as a peer support worker through a local mood disorders association. They needed someone to round out their panel of experts (perform trauma and tie a ribbon on it within the allotted five minutes), and having a job that paid more than minimum wage made me the perfect poster girl for recovery. My psychiatrist didn't know that after a long period of stability, I was experimenting with medication non-compliance and experiencing euphoric hypomania. I had my audience in stitches, including Sam, as I related some of my darkest moments sandwiched between my experience of various medications compared to street drugs and alcohol. I described Celexa's effect on me as the equivalent of one beer, and I succeeded in making the unbearable sound relatable and possibly even appealing in a way I continue to regret. It was a one act, one person performance of mental illness, and I will perform in a circus before I sit on a panel like that again. I minimized my own trauma to make it palatable for consumption. People carry on about how important it is to talk about mental illness, but there are only certain narratives they want to hear.

Namely the triumphant one. People are interested in the survivors, not the casualties. Every time there's a casualty, there's a new wave of emphasis on talking, and we start having the same stupid conversations all over again.

Like every other man I've dated, I met Sam when I was sick, but not in the stringy, unwashed hair and baggy sweatpants sense. I was sick in a way that transformed me from flat tap water to sparkling wine. Mild hypomanic euphoria can make a person seem fun to be around, and because Sam worked on the psychiatric ward of a hospital, it wasn't a feature of bipolar disorder he encountered frequently. He was versed in crisis, suicide attempts, and psychosis. Before me, all Sam knew about hypomanic euphoria was derived from class discussions and textbooks in university.

So when he invited me for coffee after the panel, presumably to discuss what peer support could offer patients, he imagined he was meeting someone like no one he had met before. I was everyone he'd met before. I'd just happened to land on a panel on a certain kind of day. I couldn't stop the charm oozing from my pores any more than you can stop the snot running from your nose when you have allergies.

It's a careful waltz of who gets to keep what when you're trying not to fight. It feels like taking apart an afghan a stitch at a time so we can each walk away with an equal sized ball of yarn, and what's yarn once you've had the blanket? There's nothing so precious Sam could leave behind to make me forget that he's taking it all.

Every married couple has too many mugs, but as a middle school art teacher, my problem is on a whole different level. If I were less sentimental, I might use each one for a week before smashing it. Sam could take every mug in the cupboard and I would never miss them, but there's a pettiness in me that wants to hold on to each one, even the *Good Morning Handsome* one I gave him for his last birthday.

So when the pettiness hits, I take a break and scour the internet for consolation prizes. Instead of growing tomatoes this summer, I'm cultivating a crop of u-line envelopes and brown delivery cartons. It's unhealthy, if not unusual, but there is one extra peculiar thing about my collection of packaging materials—it's all unopened. I haven't broken the seal on a single parcel. I figure there was a stack of presents at my wedding, so I may as well have the same for my divorce. And if I wait long enough to open them, they'll all be surprises, too.

"Are you hungry?"

It's five p.m. and this is the first thing Sam has said all day. It would be lonely if I didn't have auditory hallucinations to keep me company. For the past three nights, I've been hearing mewling kittens. No doubt a metaphor for my nonexistent babies talking back to me.

"I could eat." It's my standard reply because it's always true. I'd be down for Taco Bell after turkey dinner if you offered. Meals have been strange lately. Instead of eating together we snack a lot separately. I'm on a steady diet of crackers and pudding cups. I'm not sure my khakis will fit come August, but I'm not worried. They'll be the least of the things I've outgrown.

"I was thinking about grabbing a burger. Wanna come?"

We take Sam's car because mine is dangerously low on gas. Sam never lets the GTI dip below a quarter of a tank. He takes it to the car wash every Friday, and of course he keeps the interior tidy, too. No trash here and nothing but sunglasses in the centre console. Mine is filled with useful things like a single stick of watermelon Trident, stretched-out hairbands, wadded up napkins, and fast-food receipts. No wonder our marriage didn't last.

It's rush hour traffic, and I begin to regret my decision as soon as we merge onto Deerfoot, moving at a crawl. I didn't anticipate this much opportunity for conversation. I figured we'd just listen to each other chew.

Sam drums his fingers against the steering wheel. They are as tan as mine are pale. "Have you done any painting lately?"

He knows I haven't. He just wants to hear me say it, so I can reinforce his decision—he's not just saying yes to a future full of sticky jam-coated fingerprints, he's shaking off a failed artist. When we met I had work on exhibition at local coffeehouses, and I fared well at the night markets in the summer. He was always supportive, helping me set up and tear down the booth, promoting the events to friends and coworkers, but for the last few years, he's mostly been watching me collect the broken pencil tips of my dreams. And it's not all bad. If I painted, sketched, and sculpted because I was manic, not doing those things is a good sign, right?

Mental illness changes things. Like your aspirations. My key ambition is to stay away from the bed with restraints. Everything in the service of that goal, right down to brushing my teeth, is a form of accomplishment. It's shit most people don't keep track of, and I wouldn't either, except there are people keeping track of me. My GP and my psychiatrist. I have extra incentive to behave because I need to get my blood-work done regularly.

There's wellness and there's the performance of wellness, and sometimes it's tough to know which one I've got going on. The performance is almost a reflex, involuntary, an automatic response to people handling you like a Snow White Regency dinner plate, the kind that only comes out once a year for Thanksgiving. Every move you make is an effort to persuade them you're tough enough to survive the dinner rush at a restaurant. Am I though? And who isn't half an inch from cracking? It's exhausting, pretending not to be fragile, lest someone find out and become burdened by the weight of your fragility. The alternative is not giving a shit, and that's when they start calling you crazy. And is crazy that far out, or merely saying no, you don't get to police me socially?

I thought I was building toward that sort of emancipation with the year of *fuck it, I'm going to live.* The price of autonomy is measuring yourself out in teaspoons so no one thinks you're unstable. Freedom hinges on stability, but there are times, like now, when stability is its own kind of prison. The man I love is leaving me for a person who doesn't exist. I feel like I've earned the right to do something undignified. But if I were to go on a bender, devote a weekend to tequila and cocaine, I'd be courting an episode, and worse, I'd be giving the impression that I can't manage my recovery without my husband. So I'm trying to stay low-key untethered, the online shopping a private indiscretion between me and my credit card. No matter what I do, someone will say he left me because I'm crazy. It feels wasted, all this time I spent trying to pass for normal.

"I'm worried about you."

I stare at the tray he's holding with our hamburgers and two milkshakes. It used to be one milkshake and two straws. I slide into the booth. "Yeah, I'm a little worried about me, too." If our marriage wasn't ending, this would be the moment when I tell him about the auditory hallucinations.

"You need to get out more. Spend time with people. Get out of your head."

"So I can get more unsolicited advice? Our friends are trying to figure out who gets custody of whom, who keeps you and who keeps me. It's awful. You're the only person I talk to about stuff that is this degree of shitty."

"What about Tracey?"

My psychologist for the past five years. "She's away."

"But she'll she back soon, right?" He takes the bun off the burger and adds more ketchup.

"Probably. She's on mat leave." Saying the words feels like chewing glass.

"Are you looking for someone else?"

"I like Tracey."

"You'll find someone else you like."

"Plenty of fish in the ocean?"

Sam frowns. He's not a fan of sarcasm. "Are you working on anything?"

Does he realize he's just asked? I think of all the mailers in the garage, my workspace. "Toying with an idea for a life-size installation." I don't have to tell him it's a nursery. I'm allowed to keep certain things private. It's my duty as his future ex.

All I want is for this to be over, to get us to the vanishing point of us a little faster.

It starts to rain on the drive home. We're making a dash from the car to the house, coats over our heads, when I hear the mewling sound again. I can tell Sam hears it, too, because he stops halfway to the porch.

"Is that a cat?"

I find him huddled under the lilac bush, a scrawny tuxedo kitten with a busted abscess on his face. He hisses when I scoop him up, folding him into the hem of my shirt. I can feel his heartbeat, slamming into his ribcage, like mine does, when I meet neighbors on the street.

Inside, Sam pulls out an old towel from the linen closet. I put tuna in a bowl with some milk-soaked bread, which I place in the sink with the cat. He eats and purrs while I towel him down.

Sam watches for a minute before announcing he's going to knock on doors to see if anyone is missing a kitten. We both know that's not the case, judging by the open sore on its face. I've never felt more divorced than in this moment. Over the years, Sam and I have rescued our share of strays. Once, we even found a wounded carrier pigeon we managed to save. His departure now, when we would normally be comforting this animal together, feels more final than all the neatly stacked boxes sealed with brown packing tape.

I phone the nearest vet, but the office is closed. Done with his food, the kitten huddles into a shivering ball. I know just what to do. It takes me a minute to find the right parcel, and there's a satisfaction to opening it. It's a pink plush blanket with white bunnies on it. I tuck the kitty into its folds.

Sam returns shortly, without any luck. He frowns when he sees the blanket. Lifting the corner, he asks, "Where did this come from?"

"Just something I had lying around."

"A baby blanket?"

"It was for a project."

I can tell he has questions, but I don't owe him any answers. He goes back to packing and I go back to fussing over the kitten, wrapped up like a burrito.

With the bundle on my lap, I open a new tab on my browser, scroll through advice on how to clean his abscess. I'm so engrossed in my reading and grossed out by the pictures that I don't realize Sam is next to me, holding a canvas.

"Do you think I could keep this one?"

He turns so I can see. It's one of the ugly self-portraits from my first manic episode: me wearing a red cape, on my knees, and throwing up gold stars on a black background.

"Where did you find that?"

"In the garage, beside the tarp covering all your boxes."

My mouth draws into a thin line, but I don't say anything.

Sam places a hand on my shoulder. "It's gonna be alright. You will be. Did you keep the receipts?"

Decisions can be unmade. Transactions returned. Vows undone.

I don't reply. I'm already thinking about my next purchase. I open another tab to Amazon and type cat trees in the search bar.

Love Does Not Insist

"Will you do it?" My friend Sadie looks up at me with a gleam of hope in her bloodshot eyes.

I take a gulp of water, wishing it were beer or something stronger. "Of course." Three more gulps. "It would be an honour."

"Great! I can't wait to tell Jason." She passes the baby to me and reaches for her phone.

I'm sitting on the floor in the living room surrounded by a sea of toys. Emma has just abandoned Sophie the Giraffe so she can shove her fist into her mouth instead. What is it that my mother told me about babies? *A crib and a tit, that's all they need.* As if they don't shit and formula doesn't exist. As if love and affection are just for chimpanzees.

It's a sunny afternoon in mid-May and we've just returned from a stroll in the park. The same park where Sadie and I smoked pot during French class in high school. They've replaced the rusty monkey bars with pink and purple plastic dinosaurs for the kids to sit on, and they swapped the crushed rock with ground up tires for a softer landing. Oh, how times have changed.

"So when's the christening?"

"Two weeks from Sunday," she replies without looking up from the screen. "I need you to help me figure out what to wear. Nothing fits right anymore, and everyone will be taking pictures. I need to find something flattering."

I consider the prospect of going through Sadie's massive closet only for her to decide on a grey suit and cast a glance at my watch. "I really have to go if I'm going to beat traffic out of the city."

Sadie drops the phone on the couch beside her and scoops Emma back into her arms. "I'll walk you to the car." She follows me out to the street chattering about her plans for the celebration.

"So who did you choose to be the godfather?" I ask, fumbling through my purse for my keys.

"Cody."

The keys jangle as they hit the sidewalk.

"I know he's not your favourite person, but he and Jason were like brothers growing up. We talked about someone who lives closer, but you do, and you're my choice, so I had to let Jason have his."

Did I just consent to a lifetime of birthday parties and recitals with the asshole who ruined my life? "Is it too late to change my mind? I mean, won't your sister be jealous that you picked me?"

Sadie shifts Emma on her hip. "You're not still mad at him, are you?"

I tip my sunglasses down so Sadie can see my eyes. "I will hate him until I fucking die."

When I get back to my apartment, I open a bottle of merlot and pour myself a bowl of Cheerios for dinner.

Afterward, I take the wine to the balcony and chain-smoke while I contemplate the gravity of my mistake.

On the morning of Emma's baptism, I get out of bed at five so I have time for a closet crisis while still making it to Sadie's for eight. I need something that's not black, something that will cover most of my tattoos and at least my upper thighs, and clearly, I do not go to church often enough because nothing fits the bill. The only pants I have are jeans with holes in them. I settle for a skirt that doesn't ride up when I walk, a sleeveless blouse, and a jacket that hides everything that the blouse does not.

I pull up to Sadie's house at 7:59. I balance a tray of coffee and a box of doughnuts on the window ledge, so I can pace back and forth on her step and smoke before going inside. Jason opens the door. "Did you ring the bell?"

I take a final drag on my cigarette and grind it out on the brick wall. "You beat me to it." I drop the butt inside the coke can ashtray they hide behind their porch gnome just for me. "Where's Sadie?"

"Upstairs." He motions to the Tim's box on the ledge. "For us?"

I nod. I know I chose the right skirt because I can take the stairs two at a time.

While she sits at the vanity feeding Emma, I fix Sadie's hair into a chignon. When I'm done, I hold up a mirror so she can see the back.

"Are you sure you're going to be okay with Cody there today?"

"Don't worry. We'll be fine."

"You do know you're going to have to stand up there next to him when they dump water on her head?"

"I know how a baptism works." I start threading my hair into a French braid. "Can you make sure someone stands between us?"

She catches my eye in the mirror. "Why don't you just tell me what happened? It seemed like you had something really special."

I take an elastic from the tray and twist it into place. "We did. He blew it. That's what happened."

"I see what you're doing. You don't have to protect me. Whatever horrible thing he did won't come between me and Jason."

"Let's just do the whole sleeping dog thing, okay?"

Sadie turns Emma over her shoulder and coaxes out a burp. "Honey, are you sure that dog is asleep?"

From the bottom of the stairs, Jason calls out that we're going to be late.

The itinerary is as follows: church service, baptism, barbecue. They're expecting about twenty-five people, which is pushing capacity for their little townhouse. The problem Sadie and I both foresee is that in Jason's family, the children outnumber the adults. Jason's father, Nelson, will handle the grilling, while Sadie attends to Emma, who will probably be hungry and cranky by that time. Sadie will also have to attend to her mother, who is in the early stages of dementia. Depending on the day, she may need extra support. Jason will run interference between his siblings. If the kids get out of hand, I've been instructed to Simon-Says the hell out of that shit. I have my doubts about the effectiveness of this as a plan because the oldest is nearly twelve and the youngest is barely fifteen months.

Angel that she is, Sadie has arranged for me to sit in the pew behind the one designated for immediate family and godparents, so I can avoid having my knee pressed up against Cody's for the duration of the service. As soon as I sit down, her uncle asks me if I'm married, then asks why I'm not married, and finally, if I would consider marrying him. He tells me how much I look like his dead wife and what impressive breasts she had. Finally, he asks me what I do. I tell him I'm a documentary filmmaker and he says, "So you're in Hollywood."

I stare past Cody's shoulder at Jesus nailed to a crucifix and murmur, "Something like that."

The service is merciful and brief, which I am not accustomed to because I was raised Catholic. Before I know it, the pastor is inviting me up to read. The passage Sadie and Jason have chosen is from 1 Corinthians 13, and it seems better suited to a wedding. Behind the podium I shift my weight from one foot to the other as I scan the faces in the pews before me. My eyes dart from Cody's chiselled features to Emma, squirming on Sadie's lap. She reaches her arms out to Cody, and Sadie lets him take her. He smiles his disgustingly handsome smile. The full smile. The one that reaches his disgustingly handsome eyes. His mother is Polish, and he has the deepest cerulean eyes that only Polish people are allowed to have. Like people have stopped to ask him if he's wearing lenses. His hair is cut short. So short you would hardly know it curls at the back. He looks reformed, which he is. Sadie told me he's been clean for the better part of a decade. That's no small feat for a musician.

I open the bible to the chapter and verse. They've requested the English Standard Version, which is good because it's the only copy I have. "Love," I pause to swallow my gum, "is patient and kind; love does not envy or boast; it is not arrogant or rude. It does not insist on its own way; it is not irritable or resentful; it does not rejoice at wrongdoing but rejoices with the truth. Love bears all things, believes all things, hopes all things, endures all things. Love never ends." When my gaze finally settles on him, I see his eyes are fixed on me.

The ritual unfolds without a hitch. Emma barely fusses and Cody and I stand as far apart as possible, so it's a victory for all. Sadie has arranged for me to take the photographs with the family, and I'm grateful for the task.

"Can we get one with the godparents together?" This from Nelson.

I shoot Sadie a look. She shrugs apologetically.

Cody and I manage to take our places at the altar with Emma seated on the table in front of us without speaking. She smiles for the camera like a pro while we each keep a hand at her waist to prevent her from crawling away.

"Could you move a little closer? I need to get both of you in the shot."

We both take a step closer as the baby squirms. My shoulder brushes against his arm and the smell of his Lucky Tiger aftershave makes me queasy. I can feel tremors shooting through my hand. It's the stuff of nightmares: me, holding an infant, standing next to Cody. "Hold the fucking baby," I hiss as I yank my hand back and shove it into the pocket of my jacket.

He looks down at me and arches a brow. "Can you not swear?"

"Just please hold her."

He slips his hands under her armpits and stands her up. She stomps her slippered feet in delight. The shutter trips and I breathe a sigh of relief.

"Hang on. Can we take that shot again? Your eyes were closed."

My mouth gapes open for a moment before I manage to choke out, "Sure."

"Why don't you take her this time?"

I can barely hear him say it over the blood rushing in my ears. "No."

"Brie."

I hate the sound of my name in that pitch-perfect tone that reminds me he's a talented bassist who can harmonize with anyone. The shutter trips again.

"Can we maybe try smiling this time?" This helpful advice comes from Jason's father.

We trade dirty looks and flash our best smiles for the camera. I toss Cody a wink and a smirk before leaving him at the altar with Emma. Then I go to the bathroom and throw up. It's a purge of apple fritter and memories. Ugly chunks of our teenage happiness, ended by a procedure. I don't have a stomach that turns easily. Except for those two months in the winter of 2001, when I threw up every morning.

By the time I make it back upstairs, nearly everyone has left. I'm relieved to have this time to myself before entering the chaos of Sadie's house. I'm relieved all the way to the car until I get behind the wheel and realize it won't start. I know it's the battery because this has happened several times, and I've been putting off replacing it for months. I get out so I can kick the tire and slam my fist down on the hood.

I know he's there because I can smell the citrus of the Lucky Tiger.

"You still drive this thing?"

"It's a Tercel. They last forever."

"Clearly."

I swallow what pride I have left and ask if he has booster cables. He doesn't.

Turning on my heel so I don't have to face him, I count backwards from ten.

"You know I'm not just going to leave you here, stranded."

That's what I was afraid of. I turn back to face him. "I promised I would pick up the cake."

Pausing for a moment to scan the parking lot, he clears his throat. "Alright. Why don't we pick up the cake and drop it off and then you can deal with this?"

And here I thought the photographs would be the worst part of my day. I can feel the panic taking hold again. I shove my hands back into the pockets of my jacket. How much of an asshole would I be if I refused to pick up my own goddaughter's cake?

I sigh and follow him to where he's parked his Cobalt on the street. I try not to cringe when he holds open the passenger door for me.

The interior is immaculate. It smells like Turtle Wax and Pine Fresh. What happened to the man who threw all his trash in the backseat of his Grand Am?

"Where are we heading?" he asks, reaching for a pair of sunglasses on the dash.

"Remember that little bakery on the corner of Fifth Avenue and Eighth Street?"

"Tammy's?"

"Yeah, I don't think it's called that anymore, but that's the one." A beat passes. "Do you mind if I smoke?"

"Yes."

"Seriously?"

"We're not bringing Emma a cake that smells like an ashtray."

"I'll roll down the window."

"No."

I bite down hard on my lip. My heart is slamming inside my chest. If this keeps up I'm going to need a paper bag. He glances over at me. "Why are you holding the door like that? Are you planning to jump out?"

"Maybe."

"What's wrong? I'm getting stressed out just watching you."

"Nothing's wrong. I'm fine. I just need a cigarette, that's all." My vision has narrowed to a pin dot. I unfasten my seatbelt so I can lean forward and place my head between my knees.

"What the hell? I'm pulling over if you don't tell me what's happening."

"Jesus Christ Cody! Have you never seen someone have a panic attack? Just keep driving!"

"I'm not driving to the fucking bakery while you're passing out in the seat next to me."

When I finally lift my head up, I see that we're parked at an Esso station. Cody comes out of the store with a bottle of water and a KitKat. When he climbs in, he opens the water and commands me to drink. Slowly, that's what I do. He unwraps the chocolate, breaks it in two, and offers me half. We used to share one of these every day at recess in high school. I do not need to remember this. When I'm done the water, he pulls back out onto the street.

"So how often does this happen to you?"

"Not often. Hardly ever. Not since—" I stop myself there.

"Since?"

"Never mind." I turn on the radio.

He switches it off and turns to me as we pull up to a red light. "So it's this?" He motions with his finger as if he were buying a round for the table.

I nod without looking up to meet his eyes. I just keep picking at the corner of the Aquafina label. "We're parenting together. Do you have any idea how fucked up that is?"

"We are not parenting. We're just figureheads."

"Figureheads? Is that going to be your excuse when you miss her birthday and her little league games and her pre-school graduation?"

"Why would I miss that?"

"Right. Because you're always there when people need you."

"You know I needed you, too." When I don't reply he says, "Can we forget about all that for just five minutes?"

"Easy for you."

"Easy? Are you shitting me? I remember! All the time. He, she—the kid would be nine in the fall."

It takes me a minute to realize the car has stopped moving.

"I'll get the cake."

* * *

The party is in full swing when we arrive. Everyone has gathered in the backyard, but the sky has opened up and unleashed a downpour of rain and hailstones, so the group is rushing through the back door as Cody and I come through the front. I can hear Emma wailing over the din. She knows just how I feel.

Sadie greets me with her warmest "Where have you been?"

"Car trouble," I say passing her the cake. "What can I do to help?"

"Come to the kitchen." She's halfway there already.

Cody catches my wrist. "Are you okay?"

I look down at where his hand circles the barbed-wire bracelet tattooed on my skin.

"Always."

"This is a disaster," Sadie groans as I follow her out the back door to rescue the potato salad and condiments left out on the table. I grab the lemonade dispenser and the mushy stack of paper plates.

"Please tell me you have a lot of dishes."

"Dishes?" She brings a hand to her forehead as the rain and hail pelt down on both of us. "I don't even have room for people to sit in there."

"People don't care as long as they can eat."

"I've got raw hamburgers and potato salad soup."

"Order pizza and send someone on a run to get paper plates."

Nelson meets us at the back door with a shrieking Emma. "She needs her mom."

Sadie looks back at me. Someone pops a balloon.

"I've got it."

I dial Domino's and commission Nelson to pick up Dixie plates. Cody throws me a dish towel and miraculously, I catch it. As I'm wringing out my hair, I hear a crash, followed by a wail. When I get to the living room, I see that Sadie's plant stand, which runs the length of the picture window, is on the floor and a small body is pinned underneath, buried in an avalanche of dirt and ferns. Several people rush forward to free the little boy as his mother pushes her way through the crowd. I look over at Jason, standing three feet away with a hand over his mouth.

"You need to call this."

Slowly, everyone files out the front door and the pizza arrives as if on cue. Jason pays while Cody and I right the plants and salvage as much of the dirt as possible. "You know you can go change. I've got this."

I take the olive branch, grab one of Sadie's hoodies off the hook at the back door and head upstairs to the en suite. It's locked. I sit down on the edge of the bed and unbutton my blouse. I toss it and my jacket in a ball on the floor. Someone coughs. I pull my head through the shirt to find Cody standing in the hall, half-turned away and staring at the carpet. He looks almost as miserable as I want him to feel.

"Jason said the vacuum is up here."

"In there," I point to the closet.

He slides open the accordion doors and a tennis racket falls out. He wrestles out the Kenmore as random stuff continues to tumble around him. The electrical cord is tangled up in a pair of Converse.

"You should probably check the bag. Sadie never changes it."

"Good to know." He opens the compartment to reveal a bag that's ready to explode.

"Top shelf," I say before he can even ask.

Silence expands between us like red wine soaking into white carpet as he replaces the bag. He looks up to find me studying him.

"What?"

"Nothing."

"Tell me."

"You know, after you left that night, I started to hemorrhage. I had to take a cab to the hospital. I passed out in the backseat. The driver had to carry me in."

He leaves the vacuum and sits down on the bed beside me. "I know."

"How?"

"Your brother told me. After he gave me a black eye."

"Brian punched you?"

He shrugs. "Well-earned."

"Where were you anyway?"

"Does it really matter now?"

I bunch a handful of the quilt into my fist, clenching and un-clenching. "Yes. It does. A lot. To me."

"I went," he draws in a breath, "to meet my dealer. I needed something to get me through the night."

"*You* needed something?"

"Yeah, I thought so. At the time."

I stand up and go to the window.

He sighs. "I ended up just going to the park. You know, the one nearby with the tetanus-shot monkey bars."

"The monkey bars are gone. So is the seesaw and the tire swings. It's totally gentrified. Kids aren't even allowed to get grass stains anymore."

"Okay." He sounds confused. "Well, when I got home you were gone, and I panicked. So I called Brian."

"And he was at the hospital."

"Yeah. That's where he punched me. I was there, too."

I swallow. It feels like there's a wire coat hanger stuck in my throat. "You know you don't have to tell me this."

He joins me at the window. "I've been waiting ten years to tell you this."

All I can do is stare out at the bleeding-hearts in the garden.

"I didn't want you to have it."

"I know. We agreed."

"No." His voice drops and the cadence changes. "I didn't want you to have the abortion." There's a long pause. "And I couldn't ask you not to do it."

I turn to face him. "Why?"

The door to the en suite opens and a little boy in a Superman T-shirt comes out. He looks back and forth from me to Cody. "Have you seen my mom?"

We exchange looks because neither one of us knows who this kid is or who he belongs to, but we both know they've already left.

Cody puts out his hand. "Do you like pizza?"

I drag the vacuum downstairs to the living room to find Cody reading on the couch with the kid on his lap. I don't have the heart to ruin the moment. I also don't have the stomach to watch. Jason motions me to the kitchen, grabs a bottle of Jack off the counter, and sets two whiskey tumblers on the table. He toasts to *the best godparents Emma could want,* and I try not to choke. "It's good to see the two of you getting along."

Jason's sister comes to collect her son. The dirt gets cleaned up and the plant stand goes in pieces to the dumpster in the alley. Finally, the four of us gather in the kitchen for pizza. I hesitate for a moment at the table, trying to decide which is worse, sitting beside Cody or facing him. Ultimately, he decides by pulling out a chair for me and taking the seat next to mine. Sadie is watching me carefully and switches the topic every time Jason mentions something about old times. He takes the hint and asks me about work. Using the fewest number of words possible, I describe my latest film about the wedding industry. Sadie jumps in with details about all her favourite parts, and Cody mentions the segment on the chapels in Vegas.

"You saw it?"

"I see all your work."

"I think I hear Emma," Sadie says pushing away her plate.

"I've got it." I stand up so fast I almost knock the chair over backwards.

Her diaper is wet, so I give her a change and sing "You Are My Sunshine," in a half- whisper so no one hears it. I draw her in for a quick snuggle before I set her down in her playpen. Sadie and I settle in on the couch while Jason and Cody do the dishes. She rests her head on my shoulder. "Thank you for being here today. I know this was really hard for you."

"You know I'd do anything for Emma."

She smiles. "I know. That's why you're her god-mother."

Jason calls from the kitchen, "Babe, we forgot to cut the cake."

Her hands cover her face as she bursts into hysterical laughter. It takes me a moment to realize that she's sobbing. "Oh my God, Brie," she gasps, "this miserable fucking day."

"Be right there," I say in my brightest outside voice, and quietly to Sadie, "It's over. It's okay."

She shakes her head and sniffs. "It's not." She takes a shaky breath. "I think I'm pregnant."

"Do you girls want cake or not?"

I squeeze her hand. "I'll stall while you wash your face." Then I stand up and yell, "Don't cut it yet! We need to get a picture with Emma."

Jason straps her into the highchair, and Cody unboxes the cake while I adjust my camera settings. He takes his place behind me so he's out of the shot just as Sadie appears. She and Jason take their positions at either side of Emma's chair and each hold up a corner of the cake. They say *cheese* at my request, and as if on command, Emma squishes her hand into the icing. I take the shot. "Why don't you just all destroy it now? Get your hands in there and—"

"Here, Dad," Sadie reaches across the chair and pushes Jason face first into the cake. He returns the favour by smearing a fistful across her cheek. I keep the shutter tripping, and for a moment, I lose myself in what this day was meant to be. When the battle is over and I lower my camera, I find Cody leaning in the doorjamb, his eyes trained on me. He's smiling.

"You are such a bad influence."

How many times did he say this before kissing me?

* * *

"Jason, do you think you could give Brie a ride back to the church? Her car is still there."

He turns to Cody. "You're heading that way, right? Do you mind?"

Cody cracks his neck and looks over at me.

"You know what? It's a nice day. I think I'll just walk."

Jason turns to the window with a frown. "Isn't it still raining?"

Cody sighs, "Come on. It won't be ten minutes. You already got soaked once today."

We walk to the car in silence. He waits for me to fasten my seatbelt before shifting into gear. He's the kind of friend who never drives away until you get inside the building.

"One of us should resign."

"Was it really that awful?"

I don't know how to answer that politely. "You know, if we told them the truth, they would probably understand."

I can see the muscle working in his jaw. "I swore to you that I would never tell anyone. I am not breaking that promise now."

The wipers scrape the rain from the windshield, and I see the lights flashing at the railway crossing ahead. It's the closest I've been to crying all day.

Cody cuts the engine. He drapes an arm over the steering wheel and rests his forehead against it.

This is almost exactly how I told him I was pregnant. He was driving me home on a rainy night, and I dropped the bomb at a red light. I found the sound of the rain on the roof comforting as the silence grew between us, and it comforts me again now as I watch the railway cars pass by in a blur.

Without lifting his head, Cody turns to me. "Hey, what was the best part of your day?"

I close my eyes for a moment, speechless. He used to ask me this every night before we hung up the phone.

"That would be a tie between cuddling with Emma and the KitKat."

His face softens a little, and the corner of his mouth lifts into a half-smile. "You always did like your chocolate."

"What about you?"

He leans back in his seat and draws a breath. "Hearing you read from Corinthians."

My hand goes to my throat, and I turn to the window. I remember the first time he went inside me, I was horrified by how much it hurt. I feel about the same way now.

"Could you start the engine? I need some air."

He obliges and opens the window a crack. I can smell the lilacs in bloom mixed with rain. It's lovely, and it worsens the ache. I start rifling through my bag for smokes and a lighter.

He groans. "Please, don't."

I flip my Bic and he takes the cigarette from my mouth and tosses it in the backseat. I slide another from the pack.

"Stop."

He reaches across the console for me, one hand at my waist and the other along my throat. His thumb grazes my jawline as his eyes search mine. He tilts up my chin and angles his head.

I can hear the horns honking behind us as I reach up for the kiss.

Miles to Inches

At first it's terrifying, then it's scary, and finally, it doesn't matter. But the space between terrifying and scary, well, it can be an inch or it can be miles, thousands and thousands of miles. And just because time has passed, perhaps even a great deal of time, it doesn't mean that you have travelled any of those miles. In fact, it's possible you have been moving in the opposite direction.

In the opposite direction of what? Your fear, of course. The fear that it will happen again, that he will magically appear in line at your till, that you will have to scan his Folgers coffee, his rye bread, and his Brut aftershave while he smiles proudly at your trembling hands because he is pleased by a job well-done. Or would you walk off the job that fast? Would you let him have your job, too?

These are the things you have given up: painting, dancing, church, school, and God. In that order.

Before you stopped going to church, one of the ladies from the choir was kind enough to give you a bookmark inscribed with the "Footprints" narrative. She brought you a casserole, too. You divided the casserole between your roommate and your German Shepherd—you also gave her the bookmark.

Looking into the window at Tim Hortons, you see his reflection staring back at you, but when you turn, he's just another construction worker wearing a green hoodie over Carhartt bibs. Solid build. Average height. Dark hair, tan skin, and a nose that has been broken too many times. No moustache. He could shave it off, no? When you look again, he's gone.

This is what you have learned: Life does not stop whether you travel in miles or inches. The conveyor belt is kinder; it moves ahead when you press a button, stops when you let go.

You watch the lives of other people inch toward you an item at a time: organic carrots, vitamin D, flax seeds, Oreos. Oreos? It keeps you focused, each beep of the scanner announcing another day that has passed in your life, another day unharmed, a day you can cross off on your calendar when you get home.

* * *

"Uh, can I get my change?"

"What?"

"My change. I gave you a twenty."

"Oh, right. Here. Sorry."

* * *

You have lost weight and sleep and friends. Friends who had the kindness to tell you what you should have done. It's so comforting to know you are the victim of your own inadequate self-defence. Didn't Oprah tell you to grab his crotch?

Everyone recommends karate. You fail to see how an increase in black belts will reduce the number of assholes. But then, assholes aren't your problem. Not knowing karate is.

Probably you should have taken it lying down. (Weren't you?) At least then you would stand a chance in court. You waited forty-eight hours to go to the police. It took you that long to decide it was a crime, even if it would be called a domestic one, as if it were baked in the oven and smelled like apple crisp.

People tell you it's not your fault (in the same breath as they recommend karate). But who is to blame for the fact that you were together for two years? The red flags were there, full mast, snapping against themselves in the wind. When he punched your laptop screen he brought you carnations. After he threw up on the couch at your birthday, he baked you a cake, and after your staff Christmas party, when he said to the cab driver *This is my girlfriend, do you want to touch her*, he—what did he do, besides sleep it off in your bed? Could you really expect him to apologize for things he didn't recall?

And still it took you forty-eight hours. Forty-eight hours, half a pack of Du Maurier Signature, and one epic cheesecake.

His next appearance is scheduled on July 22. August 15. September 1. October 8.

On the eighth, he pleads guilty—to a charge for mischief. Unfortunate that he had to drive a fist through the bedroom door you locked behind you.

Note to self: Always destroy something of value prior to assault.

He receives a fine for the damages and must agree to seek anger management counselling.

Your taxes will pay for his breathing techniques.

You are angry, so angry you would pour his Jack Daniels down his throat until he choked. Then you would smash the bottle across his nose as many times as it would take for it to break—his nose, not the bottle—and you would pour the rest of the alcohol on the wound and leave him to retch on his own blood.

Angry. But not worthy of counselling.

* * *

"Do you ever look people in the eye when you take their money?"

"Pardon me?"

"You have blue eyes."

"They're green."

"Hmm. They look blue to me."

* * *

On sleepless nights, instead of counting sheep, you worry the pages of your used copy of the DSM, wandering through the diagnostic criteria of its disorders as if it were a forest, the same forest where Hansel and Gretel nearly get eaten alive.

In developmental psychology you learned that children who survive trauma often struggle to regulate emotions and may have limited language for complex feeling states. Does Gretel have limited language for her feelings about pastries and gingerbread? Or just cannibalistic witches who fatten children for light snacking opportunities?

You tear out the page with the diagnostic criteria for PTSD, crumple it in your fist, and shove it in your mouth. You chew carefully, so you can get all the nutrition from the ink. Spit it in the wastebasket with your copy of the police report and all the victim impact statements you tried to write.

Seasons change. The heat that made you toss between twisted sheets dissipates, transforming into crisp, nose-pinching air. The apples come and go unnoticed, fall and rot on the grass. The day before Halloween, you shovel them into a rusted wheelbarrow and dump them on the garden. You doubt they have much to offer in terms of renewal. If they did, you would eat one.

A friend, one who did not recommend karate, takes the trouble of setting you up on a blind date. You concede that it is time, if not too late.

Applying mascara for the first time in eight months gives you a small to medium-large panic attack. When the heart palpitations subside and the blood has stopped rushing in your ears, you apply mineral oil to a cotton pad, wipe your eyes, and begin again.

You check the weather network before dressing. Minus eight. You pull a turtleneck from the drawer, considering the benefits of not showing. No chance of frostbite. Strong likelihood of lavender-scented bubble bath and chamomile tea. But you have committed yourself, and in turn you have been assured that he is safe. Safe as Mr. Rogers, and not at all into cardigans.

It's just what you need. Everyone tells you. And you never know, they say, he could turn out to be the Sultan of Brunei.

What would you do with a sultan? What could a sultan possibly offer? Self-respect? Empowerment? Red Bull?

You do not need a sultan. You need a harem. Victims. Concubines.

* * *

"Do you ever smile?"

"Have you ever asked a man that question?"

Turning to the man in line behind him. "Does she ever smile?"

"See, I bet you didn't know you could."

* * *

He is *sultanesque* in appearance, with his stern brow and severe mouth born to speak words into law. He behaves in a sultan-like manner. He asks questions and listens attentively to your answers. You cannot focus when he speaks. He has dark hair and tan skin. Average height. Solid build.

You talk for a long time. He seems kind and funny. You are surprised and uncomfortable.

He wants to see you again.

* * *

"What does it say?"

"Hmm?"

"Your tattoo."

"Oh. *Well-behaved women rarely make history.*"

"Are you well-behaved?"

"Do you like it when women behave?"

"I think I prefer history."

* * *

In abnormal psychology you learned that trauma can cause an increase in the volume of the amygdala while decreasing function of the hippocampus, resulting in greater fear responses and interfering with memory and learning. You wouldn't know. You're not a student. Students have to remember things. Your mission is to forget, and you are excelling. You forget your lunch, your uniform, the day of the week, where you are, what you were doing, all those stupid PLU codes. You haven't consulted the list this often since you were in training. Customers sigh and roll their eyes. You are *that* checkout line. You put all the squash through as kabocha. Why do gourds need their own discrete codes? Don't they just want to be treated as equals? Of equal value? A student might distinguish between the same and equal.

You should have majored in sociology. At least then you wouldn't have to retain the pathology of your own mind. Instead you could understand the pathology of the society in which your mind exists. Now that would be information worth retaining.

* * *

You see the sultan three times, each time enjoying yourself more than the last until he walks you to your door and you experience the terror that accompanies the fall from an elevator shaft. You don't scream, or call.

* * *

"How was your weekend?"

"Eventful."

"Really? What happened?"

"Let's see. I woke up, ate half a pink grapefruit, went for a run, perspired, showered, made eggs benny and shared it with my dog, did laundry, swept, mopped, finished a crossword—

"So you stayed in."

"Your total is $29.46."

* * *

With the Sultan of Brunei off your mind, you are free to think of other terrifying things: your future without a degree, the state of democracy, your friend's upcoming wedding. She has asked you to be the maid of honour. You do not feel honoured. Polluted, jealous, yes. Honoured, no. But there is an obligation, if not to this friend, then to the other friends (who did not recommend karate) who are all but panting with excitement for your return to normal.

You want to ask them what they expect from their Wonder Bread after it's been blackened in the toaster. Instead, you go dress shopping.

* * *

"Tell me a story."

"Once upon a time there was a legitimately empowered radical feminist called Snow White. She had a lover—not a husband—who liked to drink, and sometimes when he drank, he did shitty things. He called her a witch and threw a pot of coffee at her, and then one day when the burns on her arm had healed, he was getting drunk again and she took the bottle from his hand. He lunged for it, but she held it away, so he grabbed her instead, and she hit him with the bottle and she didn't stop hitting him until he was dead."

"Show me your arms."

* * *

In the psychology of personality you learned about resilience. Of children in fairy tales. Of children who read them.

* * *

These are the positives: it's not brown. It's not a tutu. It's not a brown tutu. Your friend has selected a royal blue corset style gown that flattens your breasts into two perfect orbs of oppression thrust up to your chin. You shove a fist into your mouth and bite down hard as the bridal assistant tightens the laces. You can feel the corset digging into your ribs, squeezing like his knees. The tiny Vietnamese assistant circles you like a hornet, fussing with the hem and raving about your beauty with Sham Wow! gusto.

You can't breathe.

You come to in front of a three-way mirror, your friend at your side, the hornet hovering nearby. Your friend wants to know if you are going to be okay with this.

Okay with panic attacks?

Okay with passing out in a bridal shop?

Okay with wearing a dress that makes you feel victimized?

Okay with the idea of a very awkward first dance with the best man if he isn't allowed to touch your back, your arms, and especially not your sides?

Or just with royal blue and the corset?

* * *

The wedding day finally arrives. The timing is impeccable. It's a month from the anniversary of when it happened, the week of your would-be graduation, and the day before your quarter-life crisis can officially begin. The ceremony unfolds smoothly. The groom is on time, no one forgets their vows, and both mothers sob uncontrollably. The reception is a modest community centre affair with the food catered by the bride's cousin and a cake made by her mother. The music is supplied by a local band.

You are too busy helping the bride with her dress each time she has to pee and obsessing over your speech to worry about what will come after. The band startles you when they begin to play. You hadn't expected this moment to come so soon.

You stare at the familiar outstretched hand, only now it isn't reaching for a quart of milk in the shopping cart, it's reaching for you. You place your hand in this rough carpenter one, ready to take it back at any moment.

"You look different without the name tag and the apron."

"I almost didn't recognize you without the pencil behind your ear."

"I know, it's my best feature."

"No, that would be the scar on your chin."

"Not many people notice that."

"I've had time to look."

"I thought you didn't look at people when you take their money."

Your mouth curves into a smile as you step under the strobe lights.

"Tell me how you got it."

The Box

He was young, and handsome, and wrong for Humanities 2201 in every other way. The course was supposed to be an in-depth study of the lives of three women painters: Emily Carr, Georgia O'Keeffe, and Frida Kahlo. I'd expected that the authentic Humanities 2201 experience would feature a middle-aged woman who wore her long grey hair in a braid, preferred acetates and projectors to PowerPoint, and enjoyed waxing poetic about all the rallies and marches she attended in the sixties.

I expected this much in the same way you expect the authentic Oahu to be waiting somewhere beyond the resort, somewhere beyond the reach of tourists—you know it's there to experience if you can just find the right guide. The guide to the authentic Humanities 2201 cannot be a twenty-seven-year-old green-eyed version of Matthew McConaughey.

His name is Professor Carhartt. Call him that.

His gender was only my first objection. My second was that I knew far too much about him already. He was a regular at Shillanne's. I knew he preferred Beck's to Stella, that he would never stoop to domestic, and that if he needed something strong, it would be single malt

Scotch. In addition to exotic beer he enjoyed exotic women. Particularly the Scandinavian types.

As he burned through the roster, calling out names, I sank lower into my seat.

"Ms. McPhee?"

I raised my hand and he gave me a once-over. "I almost didn't recognize you without your uniform."

He was referring to the awful green polyester kilt that revealed the hint of a regrettable dragonfly tattoo on my inner thigh. At sixteen, with skin smooth and taut in ways I didn't deserve or appreciate, it seemed like the perfect place for my father to never find it.

I had to clear my throat before I could speak. "You'll get used to seeing me in civilian."

He gave me another contemplative stare before returning to the attendance. I pulled my hand inside the sleeves of Bobby's shirt. I wore his clothes all the time. It only seemed fair since I did most of his laundry.

* * *

It was a night class, which meant we met for three hours once a week. Halfway through there was a ten-minute break for a cigarette, a coffee, or a piss, and all three if you could manage it. I won't lie. I thought about leaving and not coming back, but dropping one course would mean adding another, and I wasn't willing to sacrifice a schedule without Friday classes for Carhartt.

We met in the arts building, also known as the ghetto, a cinder block prison for liberal minds. We couldn't have been more segregated if a set of train tracks had divided us from the rest of campus. The Coke machine ate my quarters, and the couches they were kind enough to furnish—at the end of each hall near the stairwell so we could enjoy the draft—were covered in orange paisley upholstery that dated back to the seventies, before everything from carpets, to bathroom fixtures, to Kleenex, turned pink. I'd taken my share of naps on those couches, and I was intimately acquainted with the rips and tears and cigarette burns exposing their yellow foam. The soap dispensers in the bathroom were always empty and there was only a fifty-fifty shot at getting paper towel. The wood railings had been worn smooth from the thousands of unwashed hands gliding over them. It was the only place on campus I felt truly at home.

Carhartt dismissed the first class early, after going through the course syllabus and assigning our first reading. Later at my boyfriend's I fumed. "He has as much business teaching that class as Stieglitz!"

Bobby looked up from the reusable engine filter he was washing in the kitchen sink. "Who the fuck is Stieglitz?"

* * *

The following week Professor Carhartt gave us a quiz on the reading, and we watched a film about O'Keeffe. The week after that, he gave us a quiz about the film, and we watched another one about Carr. On the fourth week, when I was ready to go to the Dean and attack the incompetence of his class, he started a discussion—meaning he asked a bunch of lame questions, like who led a more interesting life, Carr or O'Keeffe? If they had traded lives, would they have traded artistic sensibilities as well? There was more, but I wasn't listening; I was reading Judith Butler's *Gender Trouble* for my critical theory class.

Maybe he noticed my inattention, because out of left field he asked: "Do you think Emily Carr might have enjoyed earlier and greater recognition if she had an economically advantageous marriage like O'Keeffe?"

The class was silent, except for the sound of my pencil breaking.

"Ms. McPhee? You look like you have something to say."

"Are you saying she needed a pimp?"

"No." He rolled a piece of chalk back and forth in the palm of his hand. "I'm suggesting she could have benefitted from a partner, that with greater connections she might have wasted less time as a potter and dog breeder."

"Was that time wasted, or did it inform her work?"

He sighed. "It would be impossible for it not to inform her work, but did it improve it? I have never looked at one of Carr's trees and thought she must have been an excellent dog breeder."

Chuckles scattered through the room.

"No, you wouldn't. But those trees *were* painted by a dog breeder. And if the dirty thirties hadn't been so dirty for her, would she have seen the trees the way she did?"

He scowled. "She learned how to see the trees in San Francisco, and England, and France."

"She learned how to paint in San Francisco and England and France."

"We've digressed enough. My point in suggesting her career could have benefitted from marriage is that her success was late, as is often the case for artists who don't place enough emphasis on the business aspect of their careers."

"Is there a reason she needed to marry her agent?"

"Would there be another way she could find or afford one?"

"The fact that we're having this discussion proves she didn't need one."

"Yes, benefitting from the demise of the First Nations people proved to be enough. Smallpox was in her favour."

"Are you suggesting we wouldn't know of Carr without the genocide of Indigenous people?"

"Stating. Not suggesting. Their demise was her cause, and though perhaps not her intent, her career did profit. It's a limited-edition effect. We would feel differently about Elvis too, had he lived to a ripe old age."

"You're unbelievable."

"Am I? Perhaps you can persuade yourself. Who enjoyed more success? Carr or O'Keeffe?"

"O'Keeffe."

"And which one married a successful gallery owner?"

"You can't even prove there's a correlation!"

"You're right. We can't, but we certainly can wonder. And shouldn't you when you so ardently believe an artist's work is influenced by her life?"

After class, his adoring fans swarmed and swooned over him while I shoved books into my bag. He made a point to look past everyone and asked, "Why the hurry Ms. McPhee? Are you working tonight?"

* * *

Shillanne's gave new meaning to seedy. I'm sure it was a nice place once in the same way you know your chain-smoking aunt wasn't always bitter, that some of the lines on her face came from smiling, before the Marlboro cowboy rode away with someone else. It was a basement establishment—two steps down to hell if eternal damnation was a windowless room with wood panelling. The stools at the bar were covered in the requisite green tartan. Beyond that, Shillanne's was Irish in name only. Well, not even that if you consider the spelling. The owner was some French dude, also chain-smoking, who was too cheap to change it. People didn't come for the atmosphere. They came because our happy hour specials couldn't be beat. And to torture their students.

I had been hoping he would find himself a new watering hole once he was faced with the uncomfortable reality of socializing under the scrutiny of one of his students. Apparently this was not the case. Apparently the only uncomfortable reality in this situation was mine. So I started pawning off his table to other girls, but that only worked when things were slow. And of course, he knew I was doing it.

Shortly after mid-terms he came in with a stack of papers on his arm, instead of a tall, slim blonde.

"The usual?"

He nodded. I came back with a Beck's, and as I set the beer and coaster on the table, I caught a glimpse of the course number and section on the booklets. He was going to grade my mid-term here. Under the influence of alcohol. There was a disturbing possibility that the calibre of my service would affect my grade.

I asked him if he needed anything else, a menu perhaps; he thanked me and said he was fine. He was always nicer to me here than in class, but then, aren't all men nice when you wear a kilt that ends two inches from your crotch?

When I returned with his second Beck's, I set it down and reached for the empty, but he slid it away before I could reach.

"Tell me Ms. McPhee, why have you been handing off my table to your colleagues? Have I offended you in some way?"

I poked my tongue into my cheek. "Of course not. I just prefer to avoid any conflict that might arise from our affiliation."

"You feel the integrity of our student-instructor relationship would somehow be compromised?"

"Yes."

He smiled. Not the usual mocking kind he gave me in class, this one was genuine, appreciative, and it had a hint of something else. Admiration?

"You fear your marks will suffer?"

"No, I just don't want—"

"To spill something on my lap while I grade your exam?"

I inhaled sharply. "Is there anything else I can bring you?"

"Yes, your best scotch. And one for yourself."

"I don't—"

"No, of course you wouldn't."

His smile was mocking again.

As I turned away he added, "For the record McPhee, it's good that you test better than you lie."

He gave me an A– on the exam, and some glib commentary in the margins. I argued that Stieglitz' impact on O'Keeffe's career was negligible because it was impossible to manufacture talent where it didn't exist. Beside this he wrote *Can you say Britney Spears?* I added that Stieglitz would have had a more difficult job if O'Keeffe's work had only been a great body of spatter paintings. Beside this he wrote *Did he not succeed in selling vaginas?* By the time I flipped through the entire booklet, I wished he had given me a lower grade and less feedback.

* * *

"What's your major McPhee?"

"Women's studies."

"You would choose something practical. Tell me, what do you plan to do with your degree in women's studies?"

I shrugged. "Close the wage gap. Smash the patriarchy."

"For yourself, or all womankind?"

"For humanity."

"Ah. And what is such a fierce, feminist humanitarian as yourself doing at a bar, hopping around in a mini skirt?"

"Paying for her over-priced education."

"Does such an intelligent person not have a better way to pay for her education?"

When I didn't answer right away he said, "Who is that man staring at us? Do you know him?"

I looked over my shoulder. Bobby stared back at me, what-the-fuck written on his face.

"He's my boyfr—manager." I tucked a wisp of hair behind my ear.

"I'm sorry McPhee. He's your boyfrmanager?"

I put my hands on the table and leaned in close. "He. Is. My. Manager."

He rubbed his goatee thoughtfully before reciprocating. "The. Manager. Is. Your. Boyfriend." Then he erupted in peals of laughter. Bobby made it to our table in three strides.

"Is everything okay here?"

"Perfectly. Thank you. Your charming waitress was just telling me the funniest story." He winked. "Perhaps she'll share it with you later."

It was true, I was dating my boss. I had been for a year, and up until then it was a well-kept secret. A handful of my coworkers were co-conspirators who appreciated that it needed to stay under wraps until Bobby's divorce was final. I could just imagine how Carhartt would exploit this information to annoy me. What I couldn't imagine was how I would stop Bobby from freaking out.

He followed me through the swinging doors to the kitchen. It was wing night and the smell of honey garlic with top notes of ranch dressing assaulted my nostrils.

Bobby withdrew the toothpick from his mouth. "What the fuck was that all about? Who is that asshole?"

"Remember that prof I'm always bitching about?"

"No."

"He teaches my humanities class."

"He comes here a lot. That's fucking creepy."

"He was a regular before I had to sit through his lectures. He's an ass. Not a perv."

"You know they aren't exclusive. He could be an ass and a perv."

"He's not."

"Yeah. Then what was so goddamn funny?"

"Us."

"Us?"

"Let's just say he clued into the fact that I'm seeing the manager."

"How?"

"My fault."

"You told him?"

"No, he guessed. I have to get back out there."

"Are you sure that's all that was going on?"

"Yeah, trust me, I'm positive."

Bobby hired me a couple years ago, on the spot and with no experience, but if the kilt fits, right? We really didn't get to know each other until one night after a closing shift when he boosted my car. He texted me to make sure I made it home safely, and things just sort of went from there. Sure he's thirty, but whatever. Godspeed and I will be too, one day. If I met him on the street today, I'd probably think he's just some garden variety asshole who parks his car on the sidewalk and looks good in a leather jacket, but it's like The Little Prince with the fox. He's my asshole in a leather jacket.

* * *

I skipped the next class. I had an essay about toxic masculinity and Matt Damon's role in *Good Will Hunting* that I needed to finish for Gender and Pop Culture. And of course, Carhartt stopped in at the bar afterward.

"Fancy meeting you here."

"You missed an important lecture."

"I'll get the notes."

"How is it that you find yourself fit to work, but not fit to attend class? Am I to understand your job comes first?"

"I had an assignment to finish."

"And your boyfrmanager is unable to accommodate such an occasion?"

"Can I bring you something to drink?"

"I don't know. Can you pour common sense into a Collins?"

"I've heard Long Island Iced Tea is a fine substitute."

The smile didn't reach his eyes. "You need a better job. And a better boyfriend. Tell me, is Patrick Swayze a highly intelligent species like yourself?"

"I like my job. I like my boyfriend."

"Yes, and I like Cheerios, and every blonde Barbie I bring back to my apartment likes me. People like grape popsicles, Marlboro cigarettes, and Champagne, McPhee. It's unfortunate that you *like* your boyfriend and your job."

"I'm sorry you feel that way."

"When are you going to learn that shitty liars shouldn't lie? Shall I include that in a lecture?"

"Practice makes perfect. Maybe when I'm done lying to you I'll be good at it."

"Right then. Let's practise. What would happen if you told your boyfriend you don't want to wear that skirt anymore?"

"Go to Hell."

* * *

I started counting off the weeks of class that were left. And I got quiet, too.

"Shall I take your silence as mutiny? Surely it's not assent?"

"Sure."

"Are you so exhausted from prancing around in your mini skirt that you can no longer articulate a cogent argument? Shall I have a talk with your boyfrmanager?"

"You're right. I am exhausted. From your contempt, and your bullying, and your censure. My job is none of your concern, and if it disturbs you so much, I recommend you find another place to drink."

"Did you hear that McPhee? I think it was your spine snapping into place."

* * *

Carhartt gave us an option for our final assignment; we could write a paper comparing and contrasting the lives of two artists, or we could make a statement about one of the artists through an original piece of artwork in a medium of our choice. I was more comfortable citing research than I was with clay or canvas, so it was hardly an option, but getting the paper written was proving to be a challenge. I had foolishly signed up for an English class, as well as Introductory Logic, Feminist Critical Theory, and Gender and Popular Culture. I had three papers due in as many days. Carhartt's class was low priority. Worst case scenario, I could always make him a spatter painting in the middle of the night.

And then I walked into the office at work and found Bobby screwing his wife on the desk. While Bobby pulled up his pants, I peeled off my kilt and put on my jeans. I went to the bar and grabbed a bottle of Johnnie

Walker. I dumped the whole thing on the skirt, marched back into the office, flipped my Bic and held the flame until the hem caught. I threw it in Bobby's direction and said *Catch*.

I didn't stick around to see if he remembered we kept the fire extinguisher under the desk. I stopped at the liquor store on my way home and picked up a quart of Jim Beam. I walked around my apartment with the bottle in one hand and a hammer in the other; I smashed everything that would break.

The first time I woke up, it was about eight a.m. I staggered to the kitchen for some ibuprofen, swallowed victoriously, and collapsed on the couch. When I woke up at noon I cleaned up the glass. When I woke up at four it occurred to me that I needed to be at school by six to hand in my assignment, and that I hadn't prepared one. I spent another twenty minutes on the couch with a wash cloth over my face. Finally, I staggered to the pantry. Spatter paintings would require art supplies that I didn't have, but maybe I could use food colouring. Then I saw the box.

And that's how I came to submit a package of Kraft Dinner as my final assignment for Humanities 2201. Professor Carhartt merely frowned and pursed his lips when I dropped the blue box beside the stack of papers on the desk. Apparently I was the only person who had seized the opportunity to create an original work of art.

The next week passed in a blur of exams, interviews, and come-back-baby phone calls from Bobby. In the middle of this I got an email from Carhartt. He required a dissertation for my assignment. Would I be able to meet him during his office hour on Tuesday?

I knocked on the door at ten sharp.

"Ah. Ms. McPhee. Punctual as always."

It was a tiny room, not much bigger than a closet, and it made me immediately claustrophobic because I was inhaling the scent of his cologne laced with the Colts he was always smoking outside the bar, and frankly, I preferred the smell of cat piss to cigars. The space needed a window. For fresh air and to jump out of if necessary. His desk absorbed most of the space and what remained was devoured by a shelf unit burping out art history volumes and biographies of all the great painters like van Gogh, Monet, da Vinci. It read like my survey of English Literature: the male, the white, and the dead. I couldn't see a single book about Carr, O'Keeffe, or Kahlo. Even worse, he was in possession of well-used copies of Norman Mailer's *The Armies of the Night* and Jack Kerouac's *On the Road*.

"Do have a seat when you've finished your appraisal." He removed a stack of papers from a bar stool of all things.

"Nice touch."

"Do you know why you're here?'

"Because you don't know how to prepare mac and cheese?"

"More like I don't know how to grade it."

"Which is why I'm here to defend it."

"Can you?"

He let me spend a full five minutes making an ass out of myself as I tried to explain how the mac and cheese represented Emily Carr's experience of poverty. I concluded by telling him I didn't think it was fair to turn in a puppy.

His mouth twitched, turned down at the corners. I couldn't tell if he was concealing a smile or disgust. He cleared his throat. "Word to the wise McPhee, don't attempt to compare a mass- produced item to a brilliant artist. It could be perceived as insulting."

At this point there really wasn't anything I could say.

"Of course, we know you wouldn't want to insult anyone."

"Have you finished mocking me? Because I do have other places to be."

"Have you found yourself a new mini skirt already?'

I stood up and reached for the door.

"Not just yet McPhee. In case you didn't realize, you're here because I don't want to fail you."

I turned to look at him. The expression on his face was impenetrable.

"But if you mean to pass, you will have to do something for me."

"Listen, asshole, if you expect me—" The words died on my lips. He was pulling an exam booklet of his filing cabinet.

"I want you to write me an essay in lieu of the paper you would have handed in. You have forty-five minutes."

I took the booklet and sat down again. Looked at the clock and back at him. "Is there a question or a topic?"

"Yes." He paused to give me a look so piercing I wanted to hide. "In your own words, I want you to tell me the difference between an agent and pimp."

He was young, and handsome, and wrong in almost every way.

The Encounter

I've spent all these years hoping I would never see him again. Now here I am, staring at him across the room, my face obscured by the careful arrangement of hydrangeas, Champagne flute raised in a toast to his recent engagement to the woman of his dreams. A woman who surely knows nothing of what he did to me.

You have to tell someone, that's what they taught us in school. But telling someone means admitting that it happened. That you let it happen. That somehow you thought it would never be you.

Here's what happens when you don't show up for a final exam. You fail. They put an F on your permanent transcript. It follows you around, haunts your grad school applications, an educational scar of sorts. It adds to the shame, that you couldn't just shower it off, towel down and write a few essay questions. The assault was on your body, not your mind.

So instead of towelling down, you try sleeping it off with other people. Women, men, it doesn't matter. They're all equal opportunities to form fresh scar tissue. There's no self-respect to lose. Relationships are for chumps and born-again Barbies who believe in white picket fences and SUVs. There's a shortcut to healing involving intravenous drugs, and I would have followed that path to the end if my best friend, Maggie, hadn't died on it first. Three years ago, she overdosed in the stairwell of my apartment building while I held her convulsing body in my arms. I didn't let go until the paramedics pried her away from me. Now I work at the CACTUS safe consumption site. I administer Naloxone on a daily basis. Funny how one event can shape your whole life. That asshole took something from me that I didn't even know I had, a sense of safety I'll never get back, but he gave me my job and a sense of purpose, so there's that. Is it even suffering if you don't put a silver lining on it?

That's what I like about peer support. I don't have to find silver linings when I'm talking to peers. I say that sucks a dozen times a day. I hope people come away from our conversations feeling heard. And if I fuck it up? They still get clean needles and a safe, warm place to use.

My life is pretty basic now that I'm in recovery, but I was on a different path in university. Double major in Business and English. The plan was to go into corporate law—like my mother—and all that close reading of Hemingway and Shakespeare was meant to prepare me for parsing legalese. Who knows? Maybe that's what I'd be doing now if I'd stayed in my room and studied instead of getting drunk on Jägerbombs and dancing with strangers.

* * *

Naturally, I'm not meant to be here. I'm Chelsea's naive plus one, eager for our on-and-off relationship to progress to the level of attending her cousin's engagement party. I didn't expect Christopher Chalmers, beloved paediatrician, to be the same random bearded Chris who pushed me over the bed and ripped off my underwear while I begged him to stop. Seeing him wearing a clean shave and a tux with his arm cinched around a tall, slim blonde gives me the same urge to vomit. I choke back the Champagne instead.

Did I just wish this motherfucker a lifetime of happiness with a room full of oblivious other motherfuckers by association? Is my girlfriend (can I call her that?) also guilty by association? Is everyone here condoning his behaviour by celebrating his engagement? Surely someone else at this party knows what he's capable of.

I look over at Chelsea, who has been texting for the duration of the toast. When she finally puts her phone away, she leans over and whispers. "The fiancée's a plastic surgeon you know. And she's had everything done. I'd be surprised if her fingerprints are real."

I don't know how to respond, so I excuse myself to go to the powder room. That's what they call it at a country club. The wealth is obscene. In the space of three years, I've gone from using in a Greyhound bathroom to hyperventilating in a pisser with a washroom attendant and marble counter tops. This wasn't my vision of getting clean. My vision for the future has always hinged on a past that didn't happen. Or one event that didn't happen. And now my past has caught up to me, successful and triumphant, wielding power and prestige and an oversized cock.

I have a decision to make. I've been silent for a decade and I have paid with interest. Do I tell someone now? Does the washroom attendant want to hear this?

I'm running the faucet to soothe myself and taking inventory of five things I can see—white porcelain, gold taps, yellow gardenias—when I notice the attendant, a redhead with bangs, approaching in the mirror.

"Are you alright?"

"Yeah. Just, uh, having some trouble breathing."

She points to my purse. "Do you have an inhaler?"

I can barely hear her over the blood rushing in my ears, and I sink to the floor so I can put my head between my knees.

"Are you having a panic attack?"

My vision narrows to a pinhead. It's all I can do to nod before lowering my head and bracing my arms around my legs.

She kneels beside me. "I need you to breathe in slowly with me on the count of four."

I know how to breathe. It's the easiest thing. Until you forget how. She walks me through a box breathing exercise I've practised a hundred times with peers.

The regular inhale and exhale brings things back into focus. She smells like vanilla, wears a fidget ring on her thumb, and has a semi-colon tattoo on the inner side of her middle finger. Although she's six inches shorter than me and a good thirty pounds lighter, she manages to help me to my feet. My face looks grey in the mirror.

"Thanks." I want to ask where she learned that, and to tell her that I like her tattoo, but there's something more pressing. "Can I ask you a hypothetical question?"

She shrugs. "Sure."

"If you got raped and you ran into the guy ten years later, what would you do?"

The corner of her mouth twitches and something passes over her face. I can't tell if it's a hardening or a softening, but I don't get to hear her answer because the fiancée walks in. She's wearing a demure dusty rose lace dress with a high neckline and a hem that hits right at the knee. Very Duchess of Cambridge going to tea. I'll bet I could run my car on what she spends on her ash blonde with brown lowlights.

I turn off the tap and watch from the corner of my eye as she touches up her lipstick. It's a warm nude that would make my teeth look yellow. I wonder if she bleaches her asshole. Whatever. She's the kind of girl you marry. I'm the kind you rape.

She catches me staring. I smile and offer my congratulations. They say integrity is when your inside matches your outside. But who wants to be rotten through and through?

"Thank you."

Her smile is all Invisalign and white strips, but the tiny creases around her eyes seem genuine. I open my mouth, but nothing comes out.

She cocks her head slightly, eyes narrowed. "Have we met? I'm Amber."

To match her eyes? "Riley." I put my hand out. "Congratulations. Again."

"Thank you. Again." Her handshake is surprisingly firm. Assured. Privileged.

She returns the Dior lipstick to her gold clutch.

"Have you set a date?" The memories unspool: The hand that covered my mouth. How I bit down on it. The blow that followed.

"We booked the Windsor Ballrooms in June when the lilacs are in bloom, so we can take photographs outside."

"Sounds lovely." *Shut up. Cunt.*

She gives herself a once-over in the mirror, signalling the end of our conversation.

"So how did you two meet?" *Stop.*

"In biology. Freshman year at university."

I stifle a sound at the back of my throat. It's as if he's coming inside me all over again. "You went to McGill?"

She laughs and the sound pierces my memory. I would know it anywhere because there was another person in the room. Watching. Laughing. *Dyke.*

I rush into a stall, retching. Each chunk of prime rib brings up a new revelation—she's the part I blocked out. She's the one who danced with me. The one who lured me into the dorm room. When I emerge from the stall, she's gone. The attendant stands at attention next to her cart while I splash water on my face at the sink. I scroll through my phone, trying to decide if I should call my sponsor or my friend Kevin, who could totally hook me up.

She interrupts my dilemma by offering me a travel-sized mouthwash.

I shake my head apologetically. "I don't have any cash."

"That's fine." She puts the container in my hands. "I can take it from my tips."

It's a bad night for me and business as usual for her. Instead of clean needles and Naloxone she dispenses breath mints and hand cream. I'll bet she has some good stories.

I'm rinsing my mouth when Chelsea walks in.

"What are you doing, hiding in the bathroom?"

Not are you okay, or I missed you. I frown for a second, trying to remind myself what I see in her. Aside from smack in my veins, I've never wanted anything so badly, and wanting is the key. It's all we are really. "Puking, actually. Just hanging out in case there's a round two."

Chelsea wrinkles her nose, but she surprises me by asking, "Do you want company?"

I shoot a glance at the attendant who meets my eyes briefly, before averting her gaze.

"Hey, how close are you and Chris?"

"Not that close anymore. We used to spend summers together at the cottage when we were kids."

I picture a cabin on a lake, lone star quilt over the back of the couch. "Did he ever try anything funny?"

"Funny how?"

"I mean was he handsy? Did he ever—"

"What are you implying?"

"Nothing. I just wondered if—"

"If my cousin tried to shove his hand down my pants? What kind of a question is that?"

My stomach does a somersault. "The kind you ask after you've been raped."

In my mind, this is when Chelsea takes me in her arms. Maybe her brow furrows while she pieces it together, but she gathers me up and I finally fall apart. Together we come up with a plan: We lure Chris and Amber to the cottage, bind their wrists with zip ties and cover their mouths with duct tape. Discuss in great detail what their punishments should be while drinking Champagne and eating charcuterie. At sundown, we burn Chris alive and force Amber to watch.

In reality I throw up in the sink. I'm barely finished when Chelsea pulls me up by the hair and gives me a shake.

"What the hell are you talking about?"

Of course. She doesn't believe he could do that, that there's a drunk and bearded version of him that would try to fuck the lesbian out of me. It doesn't matter. I shove her away from me. She shoves back. My fist connects with her nose. She shouts, "Bitch," before it even starts to bleed, and I hear it in his voice as she pushes me to the floor. My head cracks against the pristine tile, and somehow, the delicate attendant peels her off me. Security is there before I can stand up, and when I do, I stumble to my knees.

"We need a doctor," the security guard says.

No! I think I'm screaming but no one seems to hear. They're in luck. There's a doctor in the house.

Just like that he's looming over me again. Maybe it's the decade of hard living, or maybe there have been so many others, but if he recognizes me, I don't see it register.

Nothing. That's the answer. All this time I wondered what I would do if I ever saw him again, and the answer is nothing. I let the room spin around me while my eyes roll back into my head. I don't even try to crawl away when he reaches out to examine the wound.

"She needs stitches. Take her to the hospital."

Chelsea refuses to drive me—and to be fair her nose is still bleeding—so I ask the attendant if she can help me get an Uber. She gives me a look I don't know how to read and unbuttons her vest, shrugs it off and tosses it on the counter. She guides me through the parking lot to a purple Camry with a gold door on the passenger side, helps me in and does my seatbelt.

As she drives, she talks. Asks my name, if I know the date, and when I don't answer, she blasts the radio and rolls down the windows. My eyelids are heavy. She snaps her fingers.

"I need you to stay with me."

How many times have I said that as I fill a syringe with Naloxone and jab the needle into someone's thigh?

As I cling to consciousness the same thoughts pulse in time with the throbbing at my temple: He raped me. She watched. No one believes me.

At the hospital we sit on hard plastic chairs in the waiting area where I rock back and forth to soothe myself. Eventually a nurse calls my name and leads me to another area where I lie on a gurney and stare at the fluorescent lights on the ceiling. He draws the curtain and fires a series of questions at me about what happened. I mumble incoherent answers and the washroom attendant explains everything. The doctor who arrives to give me stitches has a beard, and this time my scream is real. It takes two nurses to hold me down. I forget how to breathe again, and when I come to, she's gone. I watch blue scrubs and white sneakers and Crocs pass by in the space between the curtain and the floor, trying to wrap my head around what's happened, what I've done. I reach out for my phone. That's when I notice the note on the stool beside me. It reads: Me too.

A Tale of Two Recoveries

She started the notebook around the time her husband died, which was too soon. She filled it with stories, or titles for stories she would never write and never submit. She carried it with her wherever she went, jotted down lines nearly every day. The notebook, a blue velvet hardcover from Indigo, wasn't strictly for story ideas. She also wrote his eulogy in it, and the recipe he used to make his grandmother's biscuits, which was odd because she did her best to avoid the kitchen. She ate a lot of takeout (mostly Vietnamese) and kept assorted menus on a bulletin board in the hallway. It was old-fashioned and silly since everything was available online, like most of the journals that rejected her. She did submit. Just not from the notebook.

An Appetite for Losing. About success and how it changes you. The main character, Debbie, loses a bunch of weight through Jenny Craig and outgrows her friends who continue to enjoy dim sum without her and rock two-piece swimsuits at a weekend retreat with fat activist Virgie Tovar. It ends with Debbie choking to death on a forbidden dumpling. It would probably get rejected by a first reader, a man who can bench press his own weight and refers to his body as a temple. He has never prayed at the altar of deep-fried Mars bars. To be fair, this hypothetical man—Stephen with a p, who is only accidentally pretentious in as much as you can accidentally grow a goatee—is more interesting than Debbie and her hour-long morning runs and frozen dinners and Kyodan leggings. Debbie who is doing all this because she got tired of feeling jealous of the women on her Instagram feed. Does she know she can follow accounts that are dogs only? She could watch them do zoomies while she eats her cardboard pizza. Nothing tastes as good as smug feels. Maybe Stephen is smug and uncomfortable being called out in mediocre fiction. A line is drawn across that page in the notebook. Men don't want to read about women's body image. Women's bodies. Women. A story about misogyny? They've all been written. According to Stephen.

The Nothing That Made You. It's a good title. That's how the rejection letter would open. We loved the title, but we regret to inform you...How deep is this regret? Will there be a burial service for it, or is it more like a paper cut than a six-foot trench? Unnecessary. Like most words, her husband would say. But it could be a good story, like his, with an abrupt ending. "The Nothing That Made You" is about home. Not being able to go back. Nostalgic without being sentimental. It would make it past a first reader, maybe they even cried a little, but then it would get down-voted by the team. At a little startup. They're probably pouring their own money into it. No grant funding. They'll disappear within a year. They've spared her the arduous task of trying to get it republished. It's a favour. Well, it would be if she wrote it.

Everything That's Good in Me Seated Next to You because comparison is the thief of joy and why not spend three thousand words trying to say that? All the good stories have already been written in proverbs. Why not send rejections in the form of proverbs?

Not knowing how it's going to end. The hardest part of being married someone said. The stupidest thing she ever heard. Now there's a title for a story.

It Was Broken When I Met You. About a heart, of course. Hers if she's being honest, but who's doing that anymore? Thinly veiled fiction that never actually gets written is close enough. Akin to vows almost. How important are words you only have to speak?

Her eulogy was like that. Full of empty things people say and lies of omission. She wasn't meant to share that the alcohol poisoning that killed him had already ruined their marriage and the upholstery on the couch. All the scrubbing out puke stains and the sheer relief that it was over. Sometimes the pretending outlives the alcoholic. Problem drinker. What is the appropriate euphemism for people who drink too much, too often, and behave cruelly when they do? Hard working and devoted. That's what you say about people who are dead.

The Ones Nearest. About all the people who can't reach you. The ones who know you need help. Scratch that. Make it about asking for help that isn't there. An answer to all this "you can talk to me just don't tell me anything difficult" bullshit. Call this number to speak to someone trained to walk you through their script. Their supervisor is listening. If they deviate, they'll be in deep shit. Put your distress on their assembly line. Just don't tell them you want to die, unless you want the cops to show up at your house. They are also trained. Not to shoot you, but if they do, it will be your fault for being deranged. It's a familiar story.

She could donate the proceeds to charity. That would mean getting paid. Getting accepted. So far she has being paying for the courtesy of form rejections. "We don't make any money either," they say. As if it should make her feel better that no one is getting paid.

The notebook is full so she writes her final story on the inside of the cover.

Help Is Not for Everyone. Neither Is Recovery. It doesn't always get better. Maybe for certain people with access and privilege, but the stories they tell aren't about those things. They are about personal triumph. Which leaves her with what? Personal failure, tragedy, and a notebook, filled with carefully measured cursive curling back on itself into words no one will read.

Don't Look Back

Don't Look Back

D*ear Jesus, don't let him hug me* is my first thought when I spot him across the room. I wasn't counting on being pressed up against Liam for hours in a receiving line, shaking people's hands and accepting condolences I don't care about. I parented my mother for thirty-five years, and I'm too exhausted to cry about her death. I am not too tired to notice that Liam looks as good in a suit as he does in flannel shirts and Carhartt pants. He's six-two in stocking feet, and even in heels I barely meet his shoulder. The sheer expanse of him is vexing. Kindhearted people shouldn't come in such an attractive package.

Kindness is an underrated quality in men. We expect it from women the way we expect sap from maple trees, but in men we exact so many things that run counter to it that when it occurs it feels like a bonus instead of something fundamental to our humanity. First and last, Liam is kind. After all, he's here, isn't he? Taking time away from his family to honour my mother's memory. My mother, who barely did more than feed him Kraft Dinner and scrub Shout into the grass stains on his soccer uniform. She never treated him fairly, and yet he has nothing but forgiveness for her. Maybe I'm resentful enough for both of us.

When I was nine, my mother met the first guy I actually thought of as nice, meaning he didn't stink like booze, pass out on our couch, or stare at me in a way that made me squirm for reasons I didn't quite understand. His name was Bruce. Like Mom, he had two kids from a previous relationship—Liam and Wayne. Liam was three years older than me, quiet and gentle, basically everything you'd hope for in an older brother, while Wayne was loud and rambunctious and so much like my younger sister it was hard to believe that they didn't share DNA. There was another difference between Liam and Wayne. Liam wasn't actually Bruce's son. He was his stepson from a previous relationship, and being only nine, I wasn't informed about the why of the situation. I just knew it was complicated and that the two kids we'd eaten pizza with twice at Little Caesar's were taking over my sister's room and that Andrea was moving into mine. I was equal parts curious and unimpressed.

The first thing I noticed about Liam was that he wore glasses. I had just gotten a pair and it was reassuring to see someone older wear them with confidence. He wasn't like Wayne, throwing dirty socks in my face and leaving worms in my desk just to hear me shriek. Also, unlike most people in my life, he didn't expect me to do things because I was a girl. It was my job to wash the dishes and clear the table, but Liam always put his plate in the sink and sometimes he dried with me, which I appreciated. I soon decided having him around cancelled out all the negatives of having another younger sibling.

One day I sat down on the couch to find a slice of peanut butter toast stuck to my pyjama bottoms. That was the day I taught myself to do laundry. Taught myself because Mom was an ER nurse who worked nights, so she spent most of my waking hours asleep. At the time I just knew she was never there when I needed her, whether it was to pick me up from school after a dance rehearsal or to attend the recital.

Of course, Mom and Bruce couldn't have their perfect blended family without another baby. Soon my list of responsibilities included changing diapers and reheating bottles for another little brother, who happened to be the ugliest, crankiest baby on the planet. The colic only lasted for three months, but it felt like an eternity. Mom went back to work after eight weeks, so it was mostly Bruce doing the rocking and soothing, but I was expected to help because that's what good daughters do, never mind that I was just a kid who should have been sleeping too, like Andrea. She was six and wouldn't stir for an earthquake. Liam was the only one who could put the baby down without a fuss. He had a way of rocking him and rubbing his foot that seemed to put him in a trance. In hindsight, it was probably Liam's calmness. While the rest of us were freaking out, Liam didn't seem bothered. That attitude of *Whatever it is, I'll handle it,* is something I still admire about him.

I manage two hours in the receiving line before excusing myself to hide in the vestibule where I take a long drink from the flask I've stashed in my coat pocket. For the first time in years, I've cut back to two night caps to take off the edge, and I'm more than a little proud of myself, but if there was ever an occasion that called for the abuse of alcohol, this is it. I chew a handful of Tic Tacs and return to my station next to Liam, wishing I had my camera. It's been years since we've seen each other, even though he faithfully sends a letter each Christmas. I never write back. I plan to, but time slips by, and what am I supposed to say? I'm seeing this guy called Jack Daniels and I still don't have a family?

People expect you to hit certain milestones by the time you reach forty. People also make up stories about women who don't have children. They say that we're selfish and self-absorbed. As if generosity could only come from between my legs. As if the measure of my worth could only be my devotion to a child. It's not that I don't want that life. It's that I don't want it with anyone else.

My life is redeemed by my career. I'm a freelance photographer and I've had features in *Aperture, Harper's,* and *Vanity Fair.* There's something empowering about capturing a moment you'll never be able to get back. It makes me feel like I can cheat time a tiny bit, even if I'm stealing it for someone else. People don't take pictures at funerals, but if I could, I'd take one of Liam right now, if only because he's so unguarded. The best photos happen when people aren't posing, when you finally get to see behind the mask.

My mother always maintained that she had planned to explain it all on my tenth birthday, so when it happened shortly before I turned ten, I was eternally grateful for sex ed, and to Liam, who gave me his flannel shirt to cover the red spot on my jeans. He walked with me to the drugstore facing the October wind in his shirt sleeves because I knew my mother only kept tampons, which I was terrified to use. I picked out the cheapest pads I could find and Liam put them back and told me to find something with tabs so they wouldn't shift around in my underwear. Before his life with Bruce, Liam had four older sisters. He took some money from his pocket while I tried to steady my quivering lip and he asked if I wanted to pay or if he should. I told him I would. I was used to acting braver than I felt.

To show Liam my gratitude, I baked my first cake for his thirteenth birthday. My mother was working, and I knew she would overlook the celebration, so with the help of Betty Crocker I tried my hand at angel's food. The cake fell in the oven and I cried as if I had dropped my mother's camera and shattered the lens. Liam assured me it was okay. He even tried to persuade me that he didn't like cake that much, and when my tears subsided, he used his lawn mowing money to take me out for ice cream. That was when I made the mistake of asking if he ever heard from his parents on his birthday.

"Don't you know? My mother's dead."

"And your dad?"

"In prison."

Suddenly I understood why Liam would never cry over a ruined cake.

* * *

The best thing about this funeral parlour is the side room. It's not much bigger than a walk-in closet and it has a purple velvet love seat and a bay window with matching purple drapes. It's the perfect dedicated area to lose your shit. I'm staring out the window at climbing ivy when he finds me.

"How are you holding up?"

Today? Or for the last twenty years? I can't turn around, so I lie to the windowpane. "Hanging in there." I pause to steady my voice. "How about you?"

"Holding on."

To what? Hope? Memories? Dental floss and bobby pins? Or the perfect family progressing from year to year in Christmas cards on my fridge? I bite down on my lip until it draws a bead of blood. "How's Ian?"

It's his turn to pause. "On round three of chemo."

It's as bad as it sounds. His son is seven and has Leukemia.

I can feel him willing me to turn around, to look in his eyes and see his pain. When I don't, his hands settle on my shoulders, and just like that I'm spinning into his embrace. "I'm so sorry, Liam."

For a long moment we just stand there, holding each other against all the uncertainty of life and death, against all the unsaid words of the past and unheard prayers for the future. It's just me with my face buried in his chest, my cheek pressed against his smooth cotton shirt that smells like the Tide his wife probably used to wash it, and him with his chin resting on my head.

"Six months," he whispers. "They gave him six months."

"Shit."

"Yes, shit." He sinks to his knees and sobs against me while I cradle his head. It reminds me of the way he would hold back my hair when I threw up. He was the only one who bothered to take care of me when I was sick.

* * *

Bruce carried a five-year chip in his pocket and attended AA meetings twice a week. He talked about making amends and drank a remarkable amount of club soda, which my mother declared was only good for mixing with gin and getting stains out of laundry. Mom was a high-functioning alcoholic, and highly devoted to keeping up appearances. She poured her vodka into soda cans and dumped her empty bottles in the neighbour's recycling bin. She had us all fooled at one point or another. I should have recognized her relationship with Bruce had a limited shelf-life, and it did, but theirs wasn't the first fault line to shift. When I was thirteen, I woke up one morning to one less setting at the breakfast table.

"Where's Liam?"

My mother cast a glance at her watch. "He'll be staying with his sister."

I hadn't even known he was in touch with his siblings. "For how long?"

My mother answered by handing me Bruce Jr. "Your brother wet his pants. Clean him up, will you?"

She had a way of handing you a mop or a trash bag anytime you brought up a topic she didn't want to discuss—permission to go to a movie, new shoes, and Liam were all met with chores, so eventually I stopped asking. Bruce would only say that it was Mom's decision, which I knew, but I think it may have been what pushed him to leave. For a while they shared custody of Bruce Jr., but by the time he went to school he insisted on staying with his father. I would have liked that option, even if it meant putting up with Wayne.

***

Sitting on the purple love seat, I ask the required questions: How is Alicia coping, when did they find out, what can I do? Not well, last week, nothing. For a long time we're both quiet, which is fine. Silence has never been awkward between us. Finally, he says, "Tell me about you." I share stories about my travels, stories about exotic places and exotic food, but I include the less glamorous parts like flight cancellations leaving me stranded at airports and exotic food poisoning. He nods and listens, laughs in all the right places, and when I pause for a breath he says, "I meant did you leave anyone special at home?"

I study his face for a moment. The grooves around his mouth have deepened and there's a new crease running down his cheek, a scar. "Why did you leave without saying good-bye?"

He sighs. "Your mom. For all her flaws, she saw it before anyone, the way we chose each other over everyone else."

"What are you saying?"

"Maybe she was trying to protect you?"

"From the one person who cared about me?"

"From making choices that couldn't be unmade."

"You're wrong. *You* were trying to protect me. She was just making sure I stayed around to raise her kids. And you're not a decision I would take back."

"Who wouldn't take back most of their decisions at seventeen? You deserved the chance to be young and stupid and—"

"In love?"

"Do you honestly think you'd have the career you do today if you hung around Sylvan Lake?"

"Do you honestly think I'd care?"

He holds my gaze for a minute without answering. He's the first to look away. My life feels like a worn-out carpet that got rolled up and tossed away, or maybe I'm a single fraying thread that has come unravelled. Scratch that. I'm the tassel on the rug that gets sucked up by the vacuum.

"You were meant for bigger things." He lowers his eyes behind the black acetate frames, the sweep of his dark eyelashes veiling whatever he doesn't want me to see.

"Bigger than us?"

"There's a whole universe."

An alternate universe where I never pick up a camera because I don't need to stop time. As much as I want to blame my mother, it's not her fault that he would never leave and I would never stay. Like I'm destined to travel, Liam is destined to be anchored in a small community. A carpenter. A business owner. Reliable and trustworthy.

I can practically see the images spilling over his memory. His pain is more than I can bear.

"I should go."

He covers my hand with his. "Please. Stay. I need not to be alone right now."

The exact words I said to him the night of my senior prom, standing on the porch in my torn dress all those years ago, the last time he saved me. To tell it straight, I saved myself by slamming my hand upward against my date's nose and kneeing him repeatedly in the groin, but I knew I was lucky. If he had been less drunk and had quicker reflexes, I wouldn't have escaped. I called my mother from the phone booth at a gas station, but she didn't pick up, so I called Bruce. Liam answered the phone, and he picked me up from outside of town. I hadn't seen him for months, not since Bruce's annual Christmas potluck, and I had forgotten how reassuring his presence could be. He took my key because my hands were shaking so badly I couldn't fit it in the lock, and he led me to the couch where he wrapped me in a quilt that he warmed in the dryer. He turned on the television and switched the channel to Bob Ross, offered to run me a bath, but I said not yet. I wasn't ready to be alone. He brewed me peppermint tea and brought me toast, which I tried to eat through chattering teeth. Eventually he tucked me under his arm, and that's how we fell asleep, with Bob Ross cooing over his happy little accidents.

When I woke up he was scrambling eggs in the kitchen. We shared them off the same plate, and before he left he dropped a kiss on my forehead.

"Will you be alright?"

I stared at the scuffed toe of his boot wondering if I ever had been. If alright was a fabric, would it be the cozy brushed flannel of his shirt, or more like his denim, worn soft and faded from too many washings?

"Will you?"

I nodded and steadied my hands against his chest before reaching up. He leaned in and drew me closer. He was the first to pull away. "Not like this."

***

The thing about siblings is they have a shared pool of memories that no one else can draw on, and even if they remember the same event differently, once that connection is lost, the memory is another candle that burned out before reaching the end of its wick. Reconnecting with a sibling illuminates the past in a way that isn't possible with anyone else. Reconnecting with an old lover is the same but sadder, because the intimacy isn't something you're supposed to recall. That's meant to be incinerated at the end of the relationship. Failure to do so is a moral shortcoming. And when a person has acted both these parts in your life, they become someone dangerous. They have more of you than any one person has the right to have.

It takes a moment to get clear on what he is asking from me, which role I'm meant to play as we cry in one another's arms. I don't know what he's going to tell his wife about all the mascara I've rubbed into his shirt, but I can finally live with the truth.

Berman

"To be clear, I don't understand what Heraclitus meant about opposites. I still need to read that shit."
—ERIN

That summer I read *Natasha* twenty times trying to figure out how it was doing what it's doing so I could evoke a similar response through a narrative told from her perspective. The problem was that I had both more and less power than she did. Basically I had more in common with Berman and I was too stupid to know it. At least that's how I read it now, when I look back on those pages, brimming with feminist defiance and misunderstanding of the agency Natasha actually had.

I was living on the top floor of a four-storey walk-up in a bedroom that was technically a closet. A walk-in just large enough to accommodate a twin bed and the three cardboard boxes that contained all my personal effects. My roommate, Amber, had a lot of sex and I didn't have a door to shut, so I spent every spare minute at the library, quietly defacing a hardcover edition of *Natasha* with copious marginalia, a dull HB2 pencil my weapon of choice.

At the time my friends were decorating their walls with Nickelback posters, meanwhile I had a massive corkboard with annotated index cards of the story's arc.

"Isn't this what serial killers do?" Amber said, squinting at the inverted question mark.

"I'm writing about one of those, too."

"No shit. It's $27.38 for the phone bill."

"Didn't we just pay it?"

"It comes every month."

I was pretty sure the utilities came every time she needed extra cash for E, but I was only paying one-fifty for the closet, so I had no complaints.

Unlike Amber, I didn't have a lot of boyfriends. J.Lo and Beyonce had confidently led us out of heroin chic, but taking up space was the least of my problems. It was my mouth that got me into trouble. My uncle had nicknamed me Bumble Bee for the invective I'd been spouting since I could speak, and I'd made up my mind in middle school that if having a boyfriend meant pretending to know less than I did, then I'd rather listen to my whole class call me a lesbian at recess. I could ring my own bell, even with guys that's mostly how I finished, and really, if Betty Friedan had devoted more time to masturbation, it would be an entirely different feminist landscape. Can you imagine what the world would be like if men hadn't benefited so directly from the sexual revolution?

Right there. That's the kind of question that caused problems. You're not supposed to ask that when a man is undressing you. But seriously, this dude tried to impress me by unhooking my bra with one hand. Make me come before you do. Maybe do it twice. *That's* impressive.

So I was single and having all the orgasms my partnered friends whined they weren't getting, and I was utterly immersed in my school work. I wanted to pursue graduate studies, and I was using the summer to get a head start on my capstone project. Beyond an MFA I had a five-year plan. I was going to give Alice Munro a run for her money, and I was going to do it before I turned thirty.

* * *

"You can't do that."

The voice startled me. It was Saturday, the library had barely opened and I was sure I was alone, leaning against the pillar, marking up the dialogue between Berman and Rufus. I looked up at the speaker. He was about my age, tall and good looking, despite the bleached hair and dark goatee. He was wearing a white and blue pearl snap shirt that I instantly wanted to borrow—I knew it would look better on me since I had tits to fill out the pockets—and by the colour of his face, I could tell he'd clocked that I was wearing my Spray Lake Sawmills t-shirt without a bra. I tucked my pencil into the book to mark the page.

"You work here or something?"

"No, but—"

"Then you can't tell me what to do."

He folded his arms over his chest. "What if everyone did that?"

He understood the categorical imperative. Good for him.

"How would you like to read a book covered in someone else's crap?"

"It's not crap."

"You didn't answer the question."

"False dilemma cowboy. Not everyone is so poor they can't afford their own copy of *Natasha*."

"So you think you're special?"

"I know it." I gave him a little shove to signal the end of our conversation, but he didn't leave. "Have you even read it?"

"Of course. Would I care this much if I hadn't?"

"I don't know. You seem pretty intense."

A librarian finally poked her head through the stacks to shush us.

"Come on." He took the book from my hands and tossed it on a shelf.

I'm not sure why I followed him. Some combination of pheromones and a desire to steal the shirt? Probably because I thought it would make a good story. While Amber collected notches on her bedpost, I was busy collecting strange experiences I hoped to weave into fiction. My young life had been uneventful in a way that troubled me as an aspiring troubled artist. How would I write without memories that tortured me? I wasn't the first young woman to underestimate her imagination.

He took me to a diner on Spadina. He must have been a regular because nobody came to take our order, but someone showed up with two plates of scrambled eggs minutes after we sat down.

He told me that he'd seen me marking up the book before and that he'd read my notes. He knew I miss-shelved it on purpose so others wouldn't find it.

"Why are you so obsessed with Bezmozgis? Are you Jewish?" He tightened the cap on the saltshaker and sprinkled a little into his palm.

"No, and not Bezmozgis. Just the story."

"Why?"

"It's a fucked up piece."

"If you think the story is effed up, what does that say about the person who can't stop reading it?"

I drove my fork into the eggs. "Doesn't it make you angry?"

"No. It's moving."

"Have you ever considered that we're empathizing with the wrong person? Berman almost makes you forget she's being exploited."

"She initiates most of it."

"She's fourteen. She was groomed."

"Don't you think she knew her currency?"

"Don't you think that's a problem?"

He shrugged. "Too bad you weren't in my English class last semester. The discussion would have been a lot more interesting."

I pushed away my plate and reached for some crumpled bills in the pocket of my cut-offs. Whatever story I thought I was chasing wasn't unfolding at this two-top.

He waved me off. "It's on me."

"I'm not in the habit of letting men pay for my food."

"Then you'll be happy to know it was on the house. I work in the kitchen."

* * *

The next time I saw him at the library he gifted me his copy of *Natasha*.

"Don't read into it. I usually sell my textbooks, but the novels don't bring much."

I quit going to the library and took my work to a coffee shop because I thought it would be weird to see him again. A week into my new routine I was rereading "Tapka," the first story in the collection, when I discovered a passage underlined in blue ink. In the margin it read: I stopped here, when I understood what would happen to the dog.

I shoved the book in my bag and walked to the diner where I took a seat on a vinyl stool at the counter and drank three cups of coffee while I waited for him to come out of the kitchen.

"I missed you at the library."

I held up the book. "Some asshole gave me his copy."

"Some asshole?"

"You never said your name."

"Brandon."

I tried it out. It had a boy band vibe I didn't like. "Nah. You're a Berman."

"What does that make you? Natasha?"

"Christ I hope not. Pretty sure she's my roommate. You should meet her. We're having a party for her birthday."

The party was being held at a loft in Yorkville. It was hosted by one of Amber's wealthier conquests, so there was Grey Goose vodka and the coke was inhaled off marble countertops. I was pretty sure it was going to end in some type of orgy. Berman was the only thing that made attending this type of event tolerable.

Amber was bounced from knee to knee like a baby, flaunting her red dress without underwear with a carelessness that made me question whether I was actually a sex-positive feminist.

I caught him staring. "You want to fuck her?"

He didn't answer.

"It's okay. Most men do."

He frowned. "Want to?"

"No, fuck her. You can say the word."

"I don't have to. You say it enough for both of us."

For a second I thought he was going to kiss me. Instead someone backed into him and he spilled his Grasshopper on my shirt.

"Jesus Erin. Do you ever wear a bra?"

"In service of the patriarchy?"

"No, like a public service. Those things are like drill bits."

He set his empty glass on the ledge and surprised me by handing over the pearl snap he wore over his T-shirt.

"You know you're never getting this back."

He draped an arm over my shoulders. "We'll see about that."

Not unless you take it off me.

A few shots and a few hours later, he did.

I brought him back to the closet and when he turned on the light he discovered how I slept. The bed was unmade and at the bottom there was an arrangement of books, legal pads, index cards, highlighters, and pens. He cleared the mattress by giving the sheet one swift yank.

In the morning I resumed my work while he slept off his hangover. When I looked up from my legal pad he was watching me.

"So why do you keep reading this story?"

"It's for my senior thesis. It's creative. I'm rewriting the narrative from her perspective."

He reached for the pad, but I swatted his hand away.

"How far along are you?"

"So far it's mostly research. I'm trying to emulate the voice and form—the opening paragraph with the short declarative sentences, the deadpan dialogue, and that final arresting image."

"But if it's her story, shouldn't the voice be different?"

"Sure. That will come through in the content. I'm just talking about the form."

He nodded, but didn't seem convinced. I half expected him to say that form *is* content when he asked, "What's it called?"

I sighed. "Berman."

"Yeah?"

"Berman. That's the title."

His face broke into a grin. "So it's about me?"

"Fuck off. It's a coincidence. I promise."

"Sure, sure," he said, sliding off my underwear.

* * *

I'd spent the previous summer planting trees and fending off mosquitoes in Northern B.C., so my primary goal that year was air-conditioning, and I found it as a file clerk for Kirkpatrick and Associates. It meant wearing a bra and stockings under my professional garb, and next to having sex, Berman liked nothing better than watching me get dressed as I complained about the oppressive significance of each item before putting it on. It was backwards porn and no sooner would I have zipped my skirt than he'd be driving me into the wall and pushing the fabric over my hips. Nothing says professional like showing up for work with tousled hair and toting your underwear in your purse.

We fell into a routine. I brought my work to the diner and he brought his books to my bed. The only source of contention in our relationship was a spiral bound notebook devoted to my thesis. I wouldn't let him read it. I'd copied the full story twice to pick up its rhythm and cadence. One day I left the closet to grab orange juice and returned to find he'd helped himself.

"That's mine," I said snatching it.

"Is it?"

Was Judas so casual?

"You can only go so far imitating another writer's work. At some point you have to find your own voice."

"I'm learning."

"Learning or hiding?" He took the book from my hands, speaking more softly. "It's not a prayer. You don't have to recite it."

I reached for the notebook but he held it above my head.

"So that's it. You're jealous. You think I should be giving you head instead of practising my craft?"

"Your craft? Pickling your brains in the holy water of David Bezmozgis isn't practice. It's procrastination. You could have written an entire book in the time you've spent on some dumb story about another writer's character. You think you're such a feminist, but all you've done since I met you is try to replicate some famous dude's work."

I almost interrupted to remind him Bezmozgis is Jewish, so the holy water wasn't apt, but I didn't get the chance. He shoved the notebook into my hands and left. But not without telling me I was a dick envier and the absolute worst.

He called twice afterward. I deleted the messages without listening to them, and I was more annoyed than surprised when I ran into him a week later, leaving our apartment with his jeans half-zipped.

"How was it?"

He winced, as if I was the one hurting him.

"Fuck off Erin."

It impressed me a little how he said the actual word. And when I think of Berman now, I like to believe I changed something in him, even if it was just a tiny aspect of his vocabulary. So what if I wasn't his Natasha with my fingerprints on everything he went on to achieve? Berman didn't alter the course of my life either. There was no murder. No new identity. I didn't change schools, or clothes, or cities. I did change my sheets and my thesis—it became a critique of the portrayal of women in Bezmozgis' work—and I graduated with honours. So maybe I do owe Berman something, but one final blow job behind the stacks at the library and a pitcher of draft would cover it. I have my own body of work now, full of Natashas and Bermans sparking off each other and living inside the minds of people I've never met. The characters you're reading about don't exist. Or maybe one summer they fucked a lot inside a closet to give you this.

Everything After

Danny and I make the trip with the urn in the back and Eddie's dog tags hanging from the rearview. It's August and the Subaru's AC is broken. My palms are slick on the wheel and I have the kind of sweat moustache that should only arise from enjoying authentic carnitas on a Cancun beach. My Lady Speed Stick isn't made for this. Neither are my nerves.

It wasn't a surprise that Eddie hadn't updated his will. We've been over for four years, as long as we were together. The real surprise came a few days ago—his brother, Danny, standing on my half-rotten porch with Eddie's dog tags in his out-stretched hand.

"Thought you might want them."

Why would I want a tangible reminder of the army that destroyed my husband?

"Thanks, that's uh, very kind of you, but you should keep them in the family."

"He wanted you to have them. It's in the letter."

I'm pretty sure I'm meant to ask about this letter, and I know I should invite him in, brew coffee and set out the stale wafers reserved for company, but I'd rather feed a live cottontail rabbit to a diamondback rattlesnake. Granted, Danny is the poor rabbit here.

I've met him only once, at the wedding. Not being Catholic, or even religious, I was unpopular with Eddie's family. Out of five siblings, Danny was the only one who stood up to say nice things in a speech. He couldn't have been more than sixteen, and he was the youngest looking grown-up acting kid I'd ever seen. It's hard to believe he's the same person towering over me, all muscle and sinew, aviator sunglasses tucked into the pocket of his white T-shirt. Thank Christ he doesn't look like his brother.

Eddie wasn't much taller than me, but he was built like a Roman gladiator, one who wore Timberlands instead of sandals. The first time I saw him I thought, *now there's a man I'd like to keep in my pantry to open pickle jars*. His biceps were the size of my thigh and there was something in his manner that told me he was used to being the most powerful person in the room. A deliberateness to the way he moved, just a fraction slower than others, communicating a self-assurance I admired.

There's one more thing Danny tells me, glancing back at his Jeep. Eddie wanted his ashes scattered over the Pacific Ocean.

The honeymoon we never took. I train my eyes on my reflection in the lens of his sunglasses so the world doesn't start to spin.

He's driving to Vancouver over the long weekend and he invites me to join him. He looks down, dark eyelashes grazing the top of his cheek, waiting for my answer. Something about the humility of the gesture dissolves my protest. I agree on the condition that we take my car and here we are with our sweat soaking the upholstery and my ex-husband's incinerated body trapped inside a black ceramic vase Danny strapped in place with the safety belt.

Such a weird feeling driving through the mountains, and not just because your ears are popping. I know it's majestic and that it's supposed to make me feel insignificant in a good way, but I grew up on the prairies, so mostly it makes me feel walled-in and claustrophobic. Eddie was the only person who knew about this.

His brother is a decent co-pilot. He brought coffee and bagels and wasn't a big talker. He asked what time I needed to be back tomorrow and if I wanted to share the driving. I said eight p.m. and no.

I'm terrified this trip will drag me down memory lane. I have been successfully compartmentalizing for a long time, and I'm pretty sure if I look back I'll turn into a pile of dog shit. Few things are more shameful than being an ex-military wife. It's like you're a disgrace to the institution of marriage and your country. I'm grateful Danny knows how to leave the forgetting intact.

"What do you do for work these days?" he asks.

"I'm a caregiver at a nursing home. Mainly I work with dementia patients."

"Right. The scrubs."

"And you're still a welder?"

"Yeah."

We lapse into a silence I fill with thoughts about how stupid I am to be taking a road trip with a man I barely know, never mind that he was my brother-in-law. I keep stealing glances at the white scar above his lip. Eddie told me its tale when he discovered the scar on my knee, the one I got the time my cousin used a slingshot to fire a piece of LEGO at me. He said he had a better story, told me how his little brother electrocuted himself chewing the cord on a lamp. I wondered what drove a kid to chew an electrical cord down to the wire, and how nobody noticed before he got to it. Eddie was eight at the time, and he was supposed to be minding his siblings, so he got the belt. What kind of parents thought two injured kids were better than one? Was it even the army that fucked him up?

* * *

I met Eddie when he came into Reddhart's looking for work boots. "The kind with the thing over the laces."

"Oh, you need a met guard?"

Eddie smothered a grin as I upsold him on a pair of insoles, and he came back the next day to ask me out, which wasn't entirely unusual because I had a girl-next-door thing happening—brown eyes, brown hair, and an irksome smattering of golden freckles on my nose. I had the misfortune of looking wholesome and well-fed at the height of heroin chic, and while I was an endless disappointment to myself, the look appealed to my customers, who were mostly young tradesman. The unusual part was that I agreed to see him.

He picked me up in a jacked-up Ram 2500 with a diesel engine. My roommate peeled back the curtain and wondered how many women had gotten pregnant from listening to its throttle. He brought flowers—pink carnations with baby's breath—and took me to a carnival where we rode the Ferris wheel, popped balloons with darts for prizes that we gave away to children, and shared cotton candy. He told me he was in the military, stationed at the base in Sturgeon County, and I decided not to see him again, peak-lipped mouth and hazel eyes be damned. No amount of pheromones could persuade me to pursue a relationship with a high-risk uniform, but on our way home he pulled over for what turned out to be an injured dog abandoned in the ditch. I froze when I saw all the blood, but Eddie didn't waver. He scooped her into the truck, tore his shirt off and had me use it to apply pressure to the wound while he drove us to the nearest veterinary hospital. We maxed out both our credit cards to pay for the surgery. No one claimed her, and Eddie couldn't have a dog in his bunk, so I adopted Lucky myself. He called twice a week to check on her progress, and soon I had a border collie and a boyfriend.

We married the week I turned twenty, after dating for eight months, and then played house for six weeks before he got deployed to Afghanistan. He came home a couple of years later, covered in scars that paled in comparison to whatever he saw on the back side of his eyelids. His pain was immeasurable. Mine was confined to the agony of trying to get help for someone who didn't want it. Standard issue crying and begging him to see doctors and psychotherapists. Making excuses for all the broken dishes and holes in the drywall. He didn't want help so badly that he decided to get rid of me. So we ended our marriage—to my relief. His addiction to painkillers worsened, and he went through a revolving door of rehab houses. Last month, he ended his life on his own terms. I'd already been mourning him for years.

* * *

"When was the last time you talked to Eddie?" Danny asks.

"About a year ago. Right around my birthday." I reach for a pack of gum on the dash and offer it to him before taking a stick. "He always remembered. Not on the day, but in the vicinity. It was special because you knew he was thinking of you, not just responding to some stupid notification on Facebook."

"Yeah, he hated that shit. I'm glad you stayed in touch."

Do I tell him that his brother usually called in the middle of the night after he'd had too much bourbon, and that I always took the calls because I was afraid it would be the last time I'd hear his voice? Did Danny get those calls, too?

"What about you? When was the last time you heard from him?"

"The night he died."

The words are punctuated by the sound of my left rear tire popping and all my questions go flying with the rubber as the car swerves towards oncoming traffic. Danny reaches out to steady the wheel and I bark that I've got it, followed by a string of curses. He flips on the hazards for me as I crawl to the nearest pullout.

I pop the hatch and reach for the spare. Danny jacks the car and when I pick up the socket wrench my hands are shaking so badly I can't get it over the lug nut.

"Let me."

He changes the tire and I pass him what he needs like some kid helping Daddy. This never would have happened if we had taken the Jeep; I'm grateful he doesn't say the words. Instead he suggests we look for a garage, but I'm adamant: Ashes, then repairs.

"At least let me drive for a bit."

I surprise myself by handing him the keys.

You learn things about a person when you spend the day trapped in a car together. In addition to smelling like Irish Spring, I've discovered that Danny is a fan of classic rock: the Eagles, Hendrix, and The Who. He's a cautious driver; he signals when we pull out of the Esso lot, and he has a discerning palate—beef jerky is the only gas station food he will deign to eat. In turn he learns that I do not enjoy classic rock, although I do know all the words to "Hotel California," and that I don't trust other drivers—he's the first person I've allowed behind the wheel of the Subaru. Eddie would have made a show of driving with his knees to get a rise out of me, but Danny is serious in exactly the way I like—moderate without being uptight. Maybe he's just considerate. Do I even know the difference? All I'm sure of is that he can drive my car anytime he likes.

I pierce the silence with a question. "What's your best Eddie memory?"

"Church beer."

"Come again?"

"After our dad died, Eddie was the one who drove us to church on Sundays. He'd drop everyone at the door and I'd stay with him to park the car. Then we'd sit on the hood and drink Kokanee until it was time to sneak in for communion."

"Nice."

A smile tugs at the corners of his mouth.

"Wait. How old were you?"

"Twelve." He flashes me the full grin. He has perfect even teeth except for a crooked second incisor that leaves the smallest gap, a tiny piece of treasure it only took eight hours to unearth.

"Such a role model."

"In his way. He always had time for me. You don't often get that from your parents in a big family."

"Yeah, I wouldn't know about that. It was just me and my mom."

"Eddie said."

"You talked often?"

"More after you split. He'd go through spells where he'd call regularly, and then you couldn't reach him for months."

"Yup."

"I feel like I let him down."

"You're not the one who vowed for better or worse."

His knuckles turn white as his grip on the wheel tightens. "He was my brother."

He was right. He had known Eddie his entire life, had never lived in a world without him. He had dibs on guilt, remorse, regret, whatever this mulligan stew of feelings was called.

"Yeah, well your brother is my deepest regret."

Even more than the abortion.

That decision was easy compared to the rest of it. I knew the limit to my martyrdom. I was not introducing a baby into our domestic purgatory. It was the real reason he divorced me.

I know. I should have told him. He only found out because he answered the phone when the nurse from the clinic called to follow up post-procedure. I knew Eddie wanted a big family like his own, but the timing couldn't have been worse. He'd found a job as a mechanic at the Jiffy Lube, and he lost it for calling in sick too much. I knew he was good at his work, but his boss needed someone reliable, someone who wasn't out three days a week with migraines.

Eddie was always saying he was one of the lucky ones, alive with all of his limbs and coming home to a wife, but he also said he'd sacrifice his left arm to get rid of the headaches. They were incapacitating. He'd drag a pillow into the bathroom and lie on the tile floor next to the toilet so he could rest between bouts of vomiting, and all I could do was change the cloth on his forehead. Sometimes I'd let the dishes pile up on the counter for days so he wouldn't be assaulted by the sound of cutlery clanging at the bottom of the sink. I could just imagine how great things would be with a baby crying.

And of course there were the pills. Always gone before it was time for his prescription to be filled. Soon I had more to fear than night terrors and migraines. My newest concern became his disappearing for "cigarettes" at three a.m. and not coming home for two days. I had enough reasons, but I was scared to upset him, which I knew I'd done when I heard the phone crash against the wall.

He grabbed me by the shoulders and pushed me to the ground. I remember thinking, *I'm so glad we have carpet.* Eddie was yelling, but I can't recall what he said. A table lamp struck me on the head; *Thank God there are no kids here to see this.* Eddie's palm smacked my face; *I made the right decision.* Finally, when his hands closed around my throat and he began to squeeze, I thought, *so this is it*. Maybe it would have been if a neighbour hadn't started banging on the door. *Thank Christ we live in an apartment*. Eddie, who had me pinned to the floor between his knees, released me and stood.

"Everything's fine. Just knocked over the bookcase."

I stared at the popcorn ceiling, trying to catch my breath and afraid to move as we both waited for the footsteps to disappear down the hall.

"One reason," Eddie muttered. "I watched innocent civilians die like cockroaches and you can't give me one reason to hope?" He spat in my face and stepped on my hand, crushing bones before walking away.

I set those broken fingers myself, and my pinkie is still wonky. I make up different stories when people ask what happened. Sometimes I smashed it in a door, or mangled it in a piece of farm equipment, but in every version it's my fault. There is never a version with a violent husband exacting punishment because my husband was in the army and he came home and he did what he was trained to do.

I must be worrying my bent finger because Danny casts a glance in my direction. "Does it hurt?"

Instead of answering, I unfasten my seatbelt, crawl into the back and reach under the driver's seat.

"What are you doing?"

"Enhancing our experience." I hold up a copy of the Counting Crows' album *August and Everything After* that Eddie burned for me before he shipped out. I couldn't bring myself to throw it away, but I also wouldn't let it enter my house.

We spend the next hour singing ourselves hoarse to "Omaha" and "Round Here" on repeat.

Suddenly I can't listen to Adam Duritz sing another word about the heart mattering more or standing up straight. I hit eject. "Were you with him?"

"The less you know the better."

"So you were."

"Like I said."

I want to reach over and take off his sunglasses so I can read his face. "I had an abortion."

"I know," he says, eyes never leaving the road.

"Do you think I'm terrible?"

The rush of memories that could have occupied the pause that follows is choked out by the realization that Danny talks as carefully as he drives. He leaves a space cushion between words.

"Hurting a person isn't the same as killing them. You didn't kill anyone."

* * *

We arrive at the beach at sunset. It's deserted. Just logs and seaweed washed up on the sand and ocean and mountains meeting on the horizon under a sky streaked with pinks and orange. Seems poetic. The only kind of justice Eddie will get.

We pause at the shoreline, listening to the waves crash against the beach.

"What now?"

I take off my shoes, reach for the urn and wade in. He follows.

"Wait. This is far enough," he says when the waves start to lap against my chest. It isn't though, and it never will be. For a second I wonder what it would be like to just keep walking, but I can feel Danny's hand on my shoulder, squeezing. I hand him the urn.

"Should we say something?"

I gather a clump of ashes in my wet hand and lob it like a kid throwing a fistful of sand. "I am so fucking sorry."

Danny scoops out a handful. His voice is so soft I can barely hear. "One day closer until I see you again. I miss you already." The tenderness. I've been stung by wasps that hurt less.

One fistful at a time we set Eddie free, until finally, the urn is empty. Danny raps his knuckles against it. "What do we do with this?"

"I have an idea."

On the beach we dig and dig as the sky grows black and opens up with rain. When the urn is buried Danny leans back and sighs, "Christ I hope he's happy, wherever he is."

Thunder rumbles over us and I can see the next part unfold before it happens, how we run back to the car hand in hand through sheets of rain, the doors slamming on either side, the fog we make as he peels off his shirt and tosses it in the backseat, the breath catching in my throat and the silver medal of St. Christopher glinting against his chest as we cling to life through each other. Not meant to be, but the only way.

The Beauty and the Hell of It

Liam's son died in his arms while he read *Pete & Pickles*, tears rolling from his cheeks onto the pages. His voice often faltered when reached the part about the flood, and Pete kept Pickles alive by breathing for him all night long, but that day was different. He wept from the first line to the last. Liam felt like he had been breathing for his whole family for a long time, and he would go on doing that forever if it meant keeping Ian at his side. Alicia had fallen asleep on his shoulder, and he didn't wake her up right away. She had been sleeping so little, and he just wanted another minute like this, as a family, before he had to become a father without a child.

When she did wake up, which was only a moment later, she was angry that he let her sleep, and she had been angry ever since.

He went to work the next morning. He was a general contractor and he had projects to complete, although he knew his crew could manage without him. He went because the only way he knew how to go on was to keep going. When he came home that night, Ian's room was empty except for the furniture. She had hauled everything that belonged to him, every sweet reminder of his existence, into the alley inside giant Hefty bags. On a Tuesday. Just like that. Seven years of memories swept away by civil servants in a city garbage truck. He dropped to his knees and howled, cried himself sick and spent the night on the floor, his fists curled into the fibres of the rug where he had played LEGO and Battleship with his son.

That moment could have ended things between them, if they hadn't already been over. As soon as they learned Ian was sick, Alicia wanted to try for another baby. Initially the doctors had been optimistic about Ian's recovery, and since Alicia had carried off her first pregnancy the way other women carry purses, to her the thought of another baby was something to look forward to in the dark times ahead. He had always admired his wife's confidence and optimism, but this he felt bordered on arrogance. It seemed like the worst possible timing to Liam, unfair to both Ian and the unborn child. He needed to devote everything he had to the challenge at hand, not invent new ones. But rather than argue with Alicia, he withdrew. And when he saw Kayleigh at her mother's funeral, he began to wonder how much there actually was to be withdrawn. To make matters worse, Alicia believed the power of their positive thinking could heal Ian. Good vibrations and shit like that. Liam had to insist on the chemotherapy. She never said it, but he knew she believed it was his pessimism that killed their son.

He had thought lasting marriages were based on compatibility, something he imagined he and Kayleigh didn't have, but as Ian grew sicker and his relationship with Alicia grew more strained, he began to question what he actually knew about himself and his wife. What did anyone know of compatibility until for better or worse turned worse? He had thought it was as simple as matching socks—argyle meets argyle and you're pair bonded for life, but everyone knows what happens to socks in the washing machine. The thing about marriage, Liam realized, is that you have to keep choosing your partner over and over. It was the beauty and the hell of it.

In the end it was Alicia who packed her suitcase, but if you asked Liam, which no one did, it was entirely his fault. He may have been a dutiful husband, but Alicia had always suspected what he resisted admitting to himself. He knew that she knew because she tried to burn the sympathy card from Kayleigh before he could read it, and the sense of betrayal this evoked was second only to what he had experienced when she emptied Ian's room. It was clear to both of them who Liam was prepared to lose.

The thing about small towns is they bear witness to your changes. You watch the brick buildings fade and they look right back as you do the same. That's what he told Alicia, when she asked why he couldn't leave.

"I don't want my pain mirrored back to me," she answered, beating eggs to a froth with a whisk, far beyond the requirements for an omelette. Breakfast for supper was a Sunday night tradition in their household, but now it was the only thing she would prepare.

"Are we talking about town, or me?"

"Does it matter?'"

So their marriage ended quietly, which was the way he preferred to do things. He couldn't perform his grief at a volume that would satisfy her, but he did grieve. In the evening when he set the dinner table for three and ate alone, at nighttime when he went to his son's empty room and read *Pete & Pickles* out loud, his voice a perfect echo of the hollowness in his chest.

When it came to Christmas, Liam preferred the season to the day. December 25th always seemed like too much, so many expectations crammed into the space of a single day. Alicia had lost it on him one year because he brought home sweet potatoes instead of yams, and all he could think was how many sides do you need when you've got turkey, mashed potatoes, and gravy? It only got worse after Ian was born. His in-laws required a Christmas visit from their grandson, with no regard for the road conditions and weather, so he spent half his day celebrating and the other half driving.

Preparing for Christmas he enjoyed. He liked attending school concerts and listening to the kids sing carols out of tune and off-key. He liked taking his son shopping to find a gift for Mom, knowing full well that Alicia had hinted to Ian what she might need. He liked helping Ian write his letter to Santa while he wrote his own to Kayleigh. Staying in touch was like holding onto the sharp edge of a knife, but it would have hurt even more to let go. He looked forward to picking out a tree, decorating, and stringing lights. He loved walking Ian through the neighbourhood on his shoulders to see all the displays, loved going sledding down the same hill he'd gone to as a kid. He enjoyed bringing a bottle of Bailey's to his neighbour and drinking it in the garage while they worked on his Mustang. He liked traditions and remembering how they started and who he had shared them with in years gone by. He did not enjoy Michael Bublé, reminders of the dwindling number of shopping days, or his wife nagging him to sign cards to people he barely knew. But now that he was alone, he even missed the parts that annoyed him. He stopped observing his traditions. He didn't go to the concert to see his niece, or write to Kayleigh, or deliver Bailey's. He didn't even go to Bruce's potluck.

He wasn't expecting Bruce to show up on his doorstep on the 23rd with a pan of brownies. He gave them a sniff. The goodness was baked in alright. The corner of his mouth lifted in a half-smile. He couldn't blame the old man for trying.

"It would mean a lot if you came this year. Molly's been asking about you, even Wayne, and—"

"Alright." Liam had been studying Bruce's gaunt face and stooped posture. He reminded himself that each year they had together was a bonus. "If you can eat three of these, I'll come."

* * *

No one went to Bruce's house for his cooking. He had potlucks for a reason, and even though there would be more than plenty of other people's food, Bruce insisted on preparing his dubious chilli in his ailing pressure cooker. It wasn't Christmas without indigestion.

For his part, Liam brought pie. Mince and pumpkin. Not from the bakery, but his oven. His sisters made sure he knew how to bake, and he made time to do it every second Sunday. It was something he had done with Ian, and now it was a tradition to honour his memory. It also reminded him of Kayleigh and the times they had shared together in the kitchen doing dishes, and of course, her disastrous Betty Crocker cake. She had always made him feel cared for and included, which he appreciated. It wasn't lost on him that to her mother he was more of a guest than a family member, but Kayleigh looked up to him in a way that made him forget all of that. She made him forget everything. Even then.

The potluck was also a tradition that reached back over two decades, although Liam had missed the past two years. Ian had died on December 21st, and Liam observed the anniversary by putting in extra hours at work. He knew it was important to be with people, but for one week of the year, he allowed himself the luxury of solitude.

There was no going back from parenting. It was a threshold you crossed, and even if you took the child away and there were no others left, you couldn't uncross that threshold. You listened at night for footsteps or a cry, and when it got oddly quiet during the day, you suspected mischief. And when it was quiet all the time? You filled the silence with power tools. The sound of the Hilti drill and the nail gun were therapeutic.

In his spare time, Liam built the tree house he had promised Ian. He wanted his son to know that your word was something you kept, even once it didn't matter. It was important to him to be the sort of person Ian would have been proud to call a father. The kind he'd had in Bruce. He often dreamed of Ian getting better and playing in that treehouse with his friends, how they took their sleeping bags up there and camped out in the summer, and retreated to its shelter on rainy days. He heard their laughter and roughhousing, but he could never picture Ian's face. Whenever he dreamed of Ian, his back was always to him, usually he was running, sometimes over the bases of a ball diamond or across the street to meet his friends or even through a meadow Liam was certain he had never seen. It bothered him that he couldn't summon his son's face when all he had to do to see Kayleigh was close his eyes.

Bruce held the potluck for family as well folks he met at AA, so Liam expected to see an equal number of familiar faces and strangers. The gathering was usually held on the Friday between Christmas Eve and New Year's. This year it fell on New Year's Eve, which didn't matter that much. They weren't countdown people. It would be *Die Hard* on the television and Cheat and Spoons for card games, like always.

Bruce lived in a raised bungalow that boasted wood panelling in the basement and brown laminate flooring from the 70s in the kitchen. There was a functional milk door beside the back steps and the cabinets were original, including the giant circular hardware. Liam had offered to update the kitchen at cost, but Bruce wouldn't have it. He wasn't interested in appearances, and he maintained that everything was functional, even though the fridge leaked and he only had three working burners on the stove.

Balancing a pie in each hand, Liam rang the bell with his elbow. He wasn't expecting Kayleigh to open the door, or to flash him the broad grin that bracketed all the best memories of his youth. These days all of his interactions seemed to begin with solemn nods.

"Come in! It's freezing!"

He stepped inside and she took a pie from one hand and wrapped her free arm around his waist, hugging fiercely. "I'm so glad you came," she murmured.

It felt like someone had snapped a rubber band against his eyelids and jammed a wool sock down his throat in tandem. He wished they were alone. When he opened his eyes—he must have closed them—a pair of green eyes bored into his.

"You must be Liam."

I must be stupid, he thought as the speaker secured an arm around Kayleigh's waist.

"This is Alex."

"Nice to meet you. Merry Christmas, Alex."

Alex extended his hand and Liam gave him the pie.

"Uncle Liam!" His niece rescued him by taking a running start and launching herself into his arms. She was Wayne all over again.

Molly had just turned six and soon she would be too big for this stunt, but for the moment he just whispered in her ear, "Don't ever change."

He found Bruce in the kitchen, dumping a can of tomatoes into the pressure cooker.

"You didn't tell me Kayleigh was coming. Is that why you wanted me here so badly?"

He shrugged. "I wasn't sure she'd come."

Liam picked up the can opener and worked the lid off a can of red kidney beans. "And Alex?"

"Don't know much about him. Apparently he's some sort of editor for a magazine in Toronto."

Artsy. That made sense.

Liam sat on the couch with Molly on his lap like a sheet of armour. He tuned out the lilt of Kayleigh's voice by asking his niece about school, gymnastics, and what she got from Santa.

"Mom and Dad," she corrected him. "They do the shopping."

"Is that so?"

"Yup. Santa just takes care of the stockings."

"Ah."

"Mind if I join you?"

Kayleigh took a seat on the couch beside him, and he was reminded of their last conversation on the purple love seat at the funeral home.

"You know my uncle?"

"Sure do. Since we were kids."

Molly turned to Liam for confirmation. He nodded.

"We used to play Spoons together." She was speaking to Molly but watching him.

"I used to beat her at Spoons." He had a physical advantage that didn't factor into most card games, but they had tackled each other for the last spoon more than once. His signature move was to slam down the last spoon and send it flying so the contenders had to dive for it, which Kayleigh did every time.

"Think you still can?"

He knew he could, and that he wouldn't. His eyes wandered to Alex, holding court with his brother. "I'm afraid I've retired," he said recalling the last time she'd tackled him for a spoon. They'd gone tumbling over the back of the couch and she'd landed beneath him. He waited a moment too long to release her and they both forgot about the spoon. The spell was broken by her mother, clearing her throat. He was out of the house six weeks later.

"What does retire mean?"

He smiled at Molly. "It's what you do when you get old."

He excused himself to the kitchen. She followed.

"If I didn't know better, I'd say you're avoiding me."

Trouble. He was avoiding trouble. He sank a knife into the pie and began portioning slices onto plates she passed to him. He sighed, "You know better, and yes, I am."

A hissing noise and a rumble beside them alerted him to the danger. He dove, shielding her body with his as the lid to the pressure cooker shot into the ceiling and the contents splashed across the kitchen. When he opened his eyes, Alex was kneeling beside them.

"Are you alright?" He gave Kayleigh a hand up before turning to Liam, who had propped himself up on his elbow.

"Thanks," he said, as if it were a favour.

From the floor, Liam took in the mess around him —tomatoes, ground beef, and kidney beans sliding down the cupboards and a hole in the ceiling clean into the attic. It looked like a cross section of his heart.

Everyone had gathered in the kitchen and Bruce ushered them out before they began to argue.

"How many times have I told you to throw out that piece of junk?"

Bruce grunted. "This piece of junk has never given me a problem in twenty years."

"Twenty years? Listen to yourself! That thing is like a bomb. Someone could have been seriously hurt. We're talking third degree burns. You don't just walk away from that. We could be on our way to the ER right now."

"Are we still talking about pressure cookers?"

"What?"

"I'm sorry. I—"

"You're fine. I'm just not myself." He looked down at the tremor in his hands. He kept imagining what might have happened if Ian were there, or if Molly had been in the kitchen, or if Kayleigh had been alone. "I'll get a mop."

He lasted for another hour before retreating to the laundry room with a bottle of Lamb's Navy. He could hear the *Time-Life Treasury of Christmas* playing against the noise and laughter. He thought of his best Christmases, his first with Ian and each special one after, and perhaps his favourite one of all with Kayleigh, the look of shock and pure delight on her face when she opened the Fujifilm camera he'd picked out with Bruce. The last Christmas they spent as a family.

She found him sitting on the floor in the dark with his back pressed up to the washing machine. He was fairly certain she wasn't looking for him because she closed the door and leaned back against it and sighed before turning on the lights.

"Sorry. I didn't realize—"

That he was having a moment? For the past two years?

"Welcome to the den." He extended the bottle. She hesitated before taking it and drinking.

"God, that's awful."

"I know." He pressed the heels of his hands into his eyes before motioning to the light switch. "Do you mind, please?"

"Sorry." She returned them to darkness.

"Headache?"

"Yeah."

"I might have something in my purse."

"No, thanks." He preferred to keep his pain localized.

"This probably isn't helping." She set the Lamb's on the shelf next to a box of Tide.

"You'd be surprised." He put his hand out for the bottle. She caught it in hers and gave it a squeeze. He felt the ring, pushed his thumb into the prongs that enclosed the diamond and drew it to his chest, over his heart, where it belonged.

Acknowledgements

Please picture me delivering these words as an acceptance speech: I'm rocking a red strapless gown, the expensive kind that I don't own because it would require Spanx and dry cleaning. I'm wearing full makeup, which I blended to the best of my ability, so pretend you don't notice that my jaw is two shades darker than my neck. My voice trembles only slightly.

Thank you for reading this book and supporting a small press. This matters and so do you.

Thank you to all the talented folks at the Humber School for Writers. I'm deeply grateful to Danila Botha for two years of generous feedback and mentorship. To Alissa York for a week of the same, and to David Bezmozgis for directing all of it and orchestrating a stimulating intensive each summer.

Thank you to everyone at Guernica who laboured over this project, especially to Michael Mirolla, for taking a chance on me, and to my editor, Julie Roorda, for her keen eye and gentle hand.

Thank you to the Lieutenant Governor of Alberta Emerging Artists Awards for your support and recognition; I aim to pay it forward.

Thank you to the editors and literary journals who published earlier versions of these stories. I'm grateful to all my mentors, teachers, and peers at MacEwan and Mount Royal who have taught me about craft.

Special thanks to Laurie Hannan for the early encouragement, to Gail Sobat for my first mentorship experience, and to S. for the writerly commiseration and thoughtful commentary on these stories.

Thank you to Heather and Sana for your friendship and countless uplifting words during long seasons of rejection.

Thanks to both my families for believing in me, and knowing me at my worst and loving me best always.

Thank you Mom and Dad for not giving up on me. I hope it feels worthwhile when you hold this in your hands.

Ken and Sue, I didn't plan to write a book about sibling relationships, but that's what I ended up doing because that's how much I miss you.

Finally, deepest thanks to Myles for having faith in me and my dreams. You are the finest partner in crime that a person could want, and I love you to pieces.

Story Notables (some of these appeared with the byline Lynda Schroeders)

"Matches" an early version won the Edmonton Voices Competition, the first page was shortlisted for The Darling Axe First Page Challenge, and it was a finalist for the Writers' Union of Canada Annual Short Prose Competition for Emerging Writers.

"Jesus and Jockeys" was a winner of the Reedsy Prompts weekly contest.

"The Least Interesting Thing" received an honourable mention in the *Humber Literary Review*'s biennial Emerging Writers Fiction contest.

"Blind Date" appeared in the *Humber Literary Review Spotlight.*

"The Fault Is Yours" first page placed second in The Darling Axe First Page Challenge.

"Miles to Inches" received an honourable mention in *Room* magazine's fiction contest and first appeared on their website. It has since been republished in *oranges journal.*

"Don't Look Back" appeared in *Grain.*

"Berman" placed second in the *Humber Literary Review*'s biennial Emerging Writers Fiction contest.

"Everything After" appeared in *The New Quarterly.*

About the Author

Lynda Williams' stories have appeared in *Grain*, the *Humber Literary Review*, and *The New Quarterly*, among others. She holds a graduate certificate in Creative Writing from the Humber School for Writers and is a recipient of the Lieutenant Governor of Alberta Emerging Artist Award. Born and raised in the Eastern Townships of Quebec, she has called Alberta home since 2002. For more information about Lynda and her work, visit www.lyndawilliams.ca

Printed by Imprimerie Gauvin
Gatineau, Québec